A B-BOY'S BLUES

A PLAY IN THREE ACTS

STACY LAMAR KING

A B-Boy's Blues

Stacy Lamar King

ISBN (Print Edition): 979-8-35091-524-2

ISBN (eBook Edition): 979-8-35091-525-9

Scene

The Queen City

Time: Summer 1983

Act 1

Scene 1

EIGHTEEN

SETTING: The Gardens: A low-income neighborhood on the East Side of the Queen City. A neighborhood surrounded by two avenues and two streets, filled with the sounds of children and the hustle of single mothers. The sum of an experiment. The outcome of secret plans and wicked projects.

Which one was worst? The wicked project or the human projects that made it out of it. A riddle to everyone but a select few. The watchers.

Most of the human projects do not make it out of the project, but for the ones that do, the project still resides deep down inside of them forever.

This the watchers who watched them knew. Tracking them since the initiation of the wicked project because they knew that pressure burst pipes, yet it also made diamonds. Diamonds that come with flaws.

AT RISE: LITTLE BOY sits alone in the shade on the stoop of the three-story building that his sister LIL MOMMA had moved into. The building was officially called #480. It sat directly across from the rowhouse

LITTLE BOY called home. Its government name was #8.

LITTLE BOY sat alone on the steps with his best friend Wanda plucking her strings. He had been the recipient of the first notes to a new song. A rhythm that had no rhyme or reason. Each note a feeling. No feeling connected to another.

At the time LITTLE BOY did not know the meaning of the notes. Life would fill in the blanks. This was "His" process. Alone in his thoughts. A good thing or a terrible thing. Depending on the reason and the duration.

LITTLE BOY was still a mystery to most. He was visible. You could see him passing by. But he was rarely present. Such were his ways. Stuck in a world he longed to leave. A world he never wanted any part of.

Lost in the moment. Needing to desperately feel something. He turned his thoughts to Mika and began to play a familiar song.

A song whose meaning he understood. The notes and the emotions. He missed her so. The longing would never go away. He loved her more than life. She was filled with the light. Without her he preferred darkness.

(CAT floated down the sidewalk towards LITTLE BOY.)

CAT

Hey Little Boy. Whatcha playing?

CAT walked up the steps and plopped down on the steps right next to her favorite person on the Earth. So, close you couldn't tell where LITTLE BOY ended, and CAT began. LITTLE BOY did not flinch. CAT had taught LITTLE BOY the art of compromise.

LITTLE BOY

Hey Cat. It's an oldie but a goodie. My favorite song.

CAT

Your favorite song. You got a name for it?

LITTLE BOY

Mika.

CAT

Mika. (She paused to consider.) Is she the one that?

LITTLE BOY

Yes. She's the one.

(LITTLE BOY looked away. He refused to utter the words Mika and died.)

CAT

I like it. It has a little of everything. It's light and its heavy. You miss her a lot, don't you?

LITTLE BOY

I do. There is no one like her. She is special.

CAT

Am I special?

LITTLE BOY

Yeah, you're special. (Sarcastically.)

(They laughed together.)

CAT

Stop playing Little Boy. You know what I'm talking about. Are you going to write a song about me?

LITTLE BOY

Anything's possible Cat.

CAT

Way to make a girl feel special Little Boy. I gave you an easy ball to hit today. You were supposed to knock that ball out the park. You had one chance to make me feel like a princess today and you blew it again. You need to work on that swing. If I were you, I would write my song.

LITTLE BOY

Then pretend you're me and write it yourself.

CAT

Strike two Little Boy. You must be planning on living alone your whole life. First of all, I'm not you. Second of all, if that's even a thing, it sounded crazy coming out my mouth, I can't do what you do.

LITTLE BOY

True. If you refrain from the, if I were you talk. I will admit I have been given this gift. One I have no control of. If your song is given to me, I'll play it. It would be impossible for me not to. I play the songs given to me. That's how it works.

CAT

Little Boy the philosopher.

LITTLE BOY

Philosopher? No not me. That's a big word for such a little lady.

CAT

Big words from my big imagination. Big words are going to take me to big places.

LITTLE BOY

Do tell.

(Pinching her cheeks like her Nana.)

CAT

Little Boy, you know I hate that.

LITTLE BOY

I know, that's what makes it so funny.

CAT

I got your funny. One of these days I'm gonna give you an eye jam. Dot your eye just like the dog on the Little Rascals. Now to answer your question. I shall go wherever my heart imagines.

LITTLE BOY

Don't you mean desires?

CAT

I said imagines, I see the world through my heart.

LITTLE BOY

Not sure how that physically works but I'll roll with it. What does your heart imagine?

(LITTLE BOY chuckled.)

CAT Things I haven't seen yet. While you're laughing.

LITTLE BOY

How can you see the unseen?

CAT

How do you play notes you've never heard?

LITTLE BOY

Well played.

CAT

Do you understand me now?

LITTLE BOY

About this much.

(LITTLE BOY held his thumb and fore finger close together.)

CAT

You are just cruising for a bruising Little Boy.

LITTLE BOY

I'm just messing with you. I played a few notes to a new song right before you came over. Notes I've never known. Whose meaning I still don't understand. Each note felt like a feeling I've yet to experience. I got lost in them and couldn't find my way out. I stopped playing and then you came floating on down the avenue.

CAT

But your mind controls your fingers so your fingers can only play what it tells them to. That is how the body works. Right?

LITTLE BOY

It does to an extent. But the origin of an idea, the thoughts they are wrapped in, and the meaning behind them come from somewhere else. My fingers play notes that come from thoughts my mind never knew.

CAT

Really. (She purred like Cat Woman.) If you don't control your fingers, who does?

LITTLE BOY

I control them. It's the thoughts I don't control. I'm not sure who controls my thoughts when it comes to this guitar. Maybe it's you. Perhaps you're my new muse.

CAT

Do you think that was my song?

LITTLE BOY

I didn't say that.

CAT

Why won't he commit to anything? What's a muse?

LITTLE BOY

A person, usually a woman who is a source of artistic inspiration. (Instant retrieval from the dictionary.)

CAT

There you go sounding like Webster's again. (CAT giggled.) Imagine that little ole me, the source of Little Boy's inspiration. That would make a remarkable story. It sounds like a real mystery, and you know how much I love mysteries.

LITTLE BOY

Oh no. Not a Nancy Drew moment. How did I not see that coming?

CAT

Because you're so literal. Where do we begin?

LITTLE BOY

We, as in you and I. Begin with what?

CAT

Yes. We. As in you and me. Working together. Solving the mystery of who's putting those thoughts in your head. Because if it's me I want to know. That would change everything. My whole life hangs in the balance. Do you know how much more I could accomplish with that kind of power? Don't answer that. I'll be right back. I'm going to run and get my diary. Don't go anywhere. I'm serious you better not leave. You know how you are. Promise me you'll be here when I get back.

LITTLE BOY

Promise.

CAT

I'm not playing Little Boy. You better be here when I get back. Or there will be a price to pay.

CAT shook her fist at LITTLE BOY and ran to her Nana's house and returned in the blink of an eye. She knew LITTLE BOY was unpredictable. Here today gone tomorrow. She was as fast Mika. They ran like the wind. Watching her run made LITTLE BOY smile for a moment. He had never noticed that. He missed Mika but CAT made it easier to deal with her loss. She had appeared on the stoop on the anniversary of Mika's... She has appeared every morning since. As if she had been sent straight to LITTLE BOY. But by whom and why?

LITTLE BOY

I didn't know you were that fast.

CAT

There's a lot you don't about me Little Boy and I'm right in front of you. An open book. That's a shame. You're not the only person of mystery in the Gardens. I'm running track next year. You should come and watch me. Cheer me on. Get me pumped up. Speed is just one of my superpowers.

LITTLE BOY

Wow a superhero and a supersleuth? What shall I call you when I need help? Misty Knight?

CAT

No way. Not ever. She got her arm blown off. Don't you remember? We read that issue together. I would have seen that bomb a mile away.

LITTLE BOY

But her new arm is bionic. It's got super strength. You got to admit that's pretty dope.

CAT

Does that make it better than the original? Would you trade in your arm for a bionic one? Can you imagine yourself tick-tocking and playing your guitar with a metal arm? I'll answer for you. No. If you find yourself in trouble just call me, your better half.

LITTLE BOY

My better half? What are you talking about now?

CAT

Relax Boy Blunder. I'm not talking marriage with a baby and a carriage. That rhymed by the way. I'm talking about the better half of this relationship. This partnership.

LITTLE BOY

We're partners?

CAT

We are now. My Mom says being the better half is a lot like being a superhero.

LITTLE BOY

A mother would. What does the other half have to say about that?

CAT

You mean her sidekick? Not much. Sidekicks don't get camera time. Just blurred images. A few short lines here and there. You know this.

LITTLE BOY

I know this. I'm the sidekick now? I see where you're going with this. I don't like Better Half that is a horrible hero name. Imagine a little kid whose cat is stuck in a tree, calling for the Better Half. (LITTLE BOY laughed out loud.) How about Zippity for your new superhero name?

CAT

Zippity. Are you funning me?

LITTLE BOY

Funning you?

CAT

It's something my Nana says all the time. To be thorough in answering your question Webster style. Funnning is a source of enjoyment, amusement, or diversion.

LITTLE BOY

I don't think I'm funning you. I like Zippity. I see you zipping here. Zipping there. Zipping everywhere. Zip, Zip, Zippity.

CAT

Hold up Wait a minute. You named me Cat, and everyone calls me that. I'm having a Dr. Seuss day. I had nothing bad to say. You're not renaming me. It took a year to get used to Cat. When you need the Cat, the Cat's got your back. In the blink of an eye. I'll be there like a fly. (CAT snapped her fingers for added emphasis.)

LITTLE BOY

How about Kit Cat?

CAT

How about Cat, Cat. (Sarcastically.)

LITTLE BOY

Cat-Cat it is.

CAT

Ughhhh. You got me again. Your corny word traps. You know what I mean. Stop trying to distract me.

LITTLE BOY

From what?

CAT

Figuring out if I can control your mind.

LITTLE BOY

Why would I do that?

CAT

Because you don't want me in that head of yours.

LITTLE BOY

I was doing all that and I wasn't aware of it?

CAT

I'm not falling for your Jedi trick. I was doing all that and you weren't aware of it. Tell me what you were thinking right before your fingers played the first note to my song.

LITTLE BOY

I was sitting on the stoop. Nothing on my mind. There was no one around. Not even you, which was surprising because you're usually up at the break of dawn. The first person I see when I look out the front window.

CAT

Sir. No monologues.

LITTLE BOY

I began to daydream. Random thoughts. Where's Cat? Replaying my last B-Boy battle. Discovering the true meaning of Lettie. Wondering if the Bills will ever win the big one. The last thing I remember before hitting that first note was turning eighteen.

CAT

Lettie? That tall slim thing I saw you talking to. Is she your girlfriend?

LITTLE BOY

That's literally all you heard. Lettie is not my girlfriend.

CAT

It's not all I heard. I want to know why you were thinking about her and me at the same time? All you thought about me was why wasn't I sitting here on this stoop waiting for you like I'm some little puppy. Not pondering the true meaning of why I'm in your life. That's strike two. One more and you can beg Lettie to sit out here and wait for you. Now that it's obvious you got feelings for this chick.

LITTLE BOY

I didn't say that. I think we could have liked each other if we weren't scared of what other people would say if they knew about us.

CAT

That is the least romantic thing I have ever heard in my life. That's awful. I don't know what to call that. If I liked you, I would tell the universe about you, and I wouldn't care what anyone thought. If they did say something bad about you. It would be the last thing they said. Scared of what people think. I can't believe those words came out your mouth. Just to be clear she's not your girlfriend. Right? (CAT'S voice was a little edgy.)

LIITLE BOY had struck a nerve.

LITTLE BOY

She's not.

CAT

Good. I don't want to hurt nobody. (Whisper mode.)

LITTLE BOY

What did you say?

CAT

Nothing just writing a note in my diary. Keeping the peace. (CAT wrote the note, keep an eye on Lettie in large characters. It was the first time LETTIE'S name appeared in her diary.)

LITTLE BOY

I have never seen that. How long have you had that diary?

CAT

Since I met you.

LITTLE BOY

Really? Can I read it?

CAT

Oh no!

LITTLE BOY

Technically it sounds like I'm the main character.

CAT

There's more to my life than you Little Boy. Plus, a girl never shows her diary to anyone. Especially a boy. It's for my eyes only. So, stop trying to distract me. Your mind is all over the place as usual. Let's finish taking your statement. The last thing you remember is turning eighteen. What is the significance of that number?

LITTLE BOY

Eighteen is the magic number. I must be out of the house at eighteen. It's been in the back of my mind since I was ten years old.

CAT

Where are you supposed to go and why do you have to leave at eighteen?

LITTLE BOY

I don't know. I'm still trying to figure it out. I thought everyone had to leave the house at eighteen. I thought that was the way it was.

CAT

I don't have to leave. To be honest I don't think my parents could live without me. I can go to school and work part-time after my sophomore year or get a full-time job. Those are my options.

LITTLE BOY

Your parents have money.

CAT

Why would you say that?

LITTLE BOY

Because staying home after you turn eighteen is an option.

CAT

It is but we're not rich. We're kind of in the middle.

LITTLE BOY

You've got middle options. My options come from the bottoms, and no one wants to talk about them. I have no idea where I'm supposed to go or what I'm supposed to do. I guess the military. But look at me. I'm 5'2 and 120 pounds soaking wet. How am I supposed to run through a jungle with a pack on my back and then fight grown men like I'm Rambo? Have you watched a war movie? They're swimming through rivers and oceans. I can't float. There must be a better option. This is a lot of pressure and no one I know understands it. I'm always stressed out.

CAT

What about college? You're the smartest person I know. I thought all boys were dumb until I met you.

LITTLE BOY

I hate school.

CAT

WHAT? (CAT was shocked to hear those words.) You go to the best school in the city, maybe the world.

LITTLE BOY

It's not what you think it is. It's a social experiment and I'm tired of feeling like a lab rat. I've been there seven years looking at the same faces listening to the same ole song.

CAT

I hope you're not thinking about doing what these losers are doing in these streets. Selling drugs to our people. We know people who have killed people they went to kindergarten with. That's crazy. Drugs are not an option.

LITTLE BOY

Cat if I can't fight like Rambo. You know I can't go to prison. All they do is lift weights, fight over cigarettes and soup and turn boys into girls.

CAT

Cigarettes and soup? That's what they do in prison? For real. Where did you hear that Little Boy?

LITTLE BOY

HBO. Scared Straight the documentary. You didn't see that? There's no place in prison for me after watching that. It scared me straight. I laughed at Nancy Reagan and Gary Coleman saying no to drugs. But Scared Straight was nothing to laugh about.

CAT

I know what you mean. I saw a real live crackhead and I was done. (They laughed nervously.) Let's say you don't go to the military, you don't go to college, you don't sell drugs, and you don't go to prison. What are you going to do?

LITTLE BOY

Get a job that requires no experience I suppose. But I'm still not sure if I do that, that I can stay at home. I don't know what my options are. So many questions. But no one dares ask them because the conversation starts and ends with, I don't know what you're doing at eighteen, I don't care what you're doing at eighteen, but I do know you're getting the hell out of my house.

CAT

Wow.

LITTLE BOY

Look at me. I don't own a bike. I don't have a bank account. I don't know how to drive. My clothes come from K-Mart. How am I supposed to get to work? What am I going to wear to an interview? I hate living like this. I have nothing to offer anyone. I'm tired of being a bum.

CAT

Yes, you do. You're the coolest non-driving, no bike having, no bank deposit making, guitar playing, B-Boy battling, cutest thang that ever lived, and the smartest brother I have ever known. Maybe the right job will find you.

LITTLE BOY

Maybe money will fall from the sky.

CAT

Your attitude sucks. You do know that attitude is everything. I'm going to wish upon a star for you tonight. All you need is some help. (CAT entered a new note in her diary.)

LITTLE BOY

While you're doing that. Please wish for an explanation for why my life has been so crappy.

CAT

I'll wish for that too. So, you can get that off your mind. You can't keep all that bottled up inside you. I never knew you felt like this, and I thought I had problems. I got kid problems. You have grown-up problems but you're still a kid.

LITTLE BOY

Tell me about it.

CAT

Whatever you do I hope you don't leave any time soon. I mean I just met you and I thought we had forever. I was dreaming. I don't want to think about you leaving. That thought makes me sad. Little Boy, I have so much to write about tonight.

LITTLE BOY

I need a drink. You need one too?

CAT

Bartender I'll take mine on the rocks but not in a dirty glass. (Sounding like Mae West.)

LITTLE BOY

OK Ms. West. I'll be right back.

(LITTLE BOY went into his house to retrieve two sodas.)

CAT

Little Boy I think I've figured out who your muse is. (Shouting towards LITTLE BOY'S house.)

LITTLE BOY

Oh yeah, well tell me who you think it is when I come outside. (Shouting from inside his house.)

(LITTLE BOY exits his house and walks towards the stoop of #480 with a can of root beer for himself and a glass of root beer on the rocks for CAT.)

CAT

Ooh why don't you come up and see me sometime. (CAT was still in character. She Could drag it on for hours.)

LITTLE BOY

What's wrong with now? (LITTLE BOY joined CAT. He could improvise with the best of them.)

CAT

What's wrong with sometimes?

LITTLE BOY

Ok let's split the difference.

CAT

What's the difference? (Sassy like.)

LITTLE BOY

That's what I say. What's the difference? Kiss me you fool.

CAT

I'll kiss you when I'm good and ready. Better make that bad and ready.

(CAT couldn't contain it any longer. She blurted out laughing. She did her best Mae West strut down the stairs and over to LITTLE BOY to get her glass of soda.)

CAT

Because a good man these days is hard to find.

(LITTLE BOY laughed and handed CAT the glass of root beer. CAT took the glass and kissed LITTLE BOY on the lips. They paused, looked around and then towards the ground and finally at each other.)

LITTLE BOY

OK. How about those Bills? One day they're going to win it all, right?

CAT

Yeah, one day we're going to win it all. (Blushing.)

LITTLE BOY

I'm surprised you still remember that skit.

CAT

I know. I thought I was the only one. My Mom said Janet was acting fast. I remember saying she's walking and talking pretty slow to me. Then my Mom and Dad laughed and started whispering and never said another word about it. Parents can be so weird.

LITTLE BOY

I think fast is a code word for sassy. My Mom used to say you're acting too big for your britches when I was young. It took me years to figure that one out.

CAT

Why don't they just say sassy when they mean sassy?

LITTLE BOY

Parents love the codes. They have their own secret language.

CAT

Thanks for clearing that up Little Boy. I'm on to them now. It's curtains.

LITTLE BOY

So, who's my muse?

CAT

I don't think it's a person. Your muse is your situation. Turning eighteen.

LITTLE BOY

Why do you think that?

CAT

It's a feeling. A vibe I got from listening to you talk about it. It might not be what you want to hear, and it may not be the message your Mom wants to give to you. But it could be what you need to hear. A message given to her to give to you.

LITTLE BOY

Really? If you were a mother, would you give your child that message?

CAT

If I knew it came from above I would. Even if I didn't understand it. If my son didn't like it here, hated school, was surrounded by drugs and drug dealers, friends killing friends, and I didn't have the money to keep himself safe I would say whatever I had to say to get him out of that situation. Even if it made me the bad guy. Even if he hated me. There's a world outside of the Gardens and a better one outside the Queen City. Here in the Gardens, your world fits within four streets. A prison without bars.

LITTLE BOY

I thought my leaving would make you sad.

CAT

It does. There are levels to sadness. Nothing would be sadder than you staying here and getting caught up in a situation especially when prison isn't an option. One day I want you to sing a song about you and me. Not one about a little boy I used to know who never grew up to be the man I wanted him to be.

(CAT wiped a tear from her eye.)

LITTLE BOY

You would rather watch me leave and never return than see me stay? Why does it feel like you're choosing something other than me? No one ever chooses me.

CAT

You mean watch you suffer. Apparently, I've been doing that since I met you. You have never been happy here. If I can be perfectly honest with you, I don't know what happiness means to you. You paint the world in shades of grey. Different levels of sadness. You may never be happy like I think of it. I know you can be less sad somewhere else because I have seen that. Maybe being less sad is your happiness. Those words literally just came to me. I think that's the meaning behind eighteen.

LITTLE BOY

Maybe you're right. I don't know.

CAT

Didn't you move to Atlanta last year?

LITTLE BOY

I did.

CAT

Why'd you come back?

LITTLE BOY

I wasn't less sad.

CAT

You know three things now. Atlanta wasn't for you, neither is the Queen City, and you want to be somewhere you feel less sad. Your mind is a sea of grey Little Boy. Sad is your favorite crayon. You paint everything inside this room of yours different shades of gray.

LITTLE BOY

I didn't ask to be in this room.

CAT

I know you didn't. You can't change the room, but you can paint the room a new color when you discover one.

LITTLE BOY

How do I discover a new color?

CAT

Dance like a B-Boy. Write a new song. Tell an amazing story. Like the story of you battling a ninja and living to tell everyone about it.

LITTLE BOY

You've heard that story?

CAT

Are you kidding me? Who hasn't heard it? It's the greatest story ever told. A B-Boy battles a ninja and lives to talk about it. I love that story. It gives me so much hope. When I heard it, I had to find you. I had to meet you. It's the reason I'm sitting here. My cousin told me that story and I said I'm coming to the Gardens to find that Little Boy. I want to hear it from you. Please tell me the story.

LITTLE BOY

OK but this is the last time I'm going to tell it.

CAT

Bet. Hold that thought. Don't start yet. (CAT ran to the end of the walk and screamed towards the playground where B-Boy's came to battle. The very playground where LITTLE BOY stood his ground against a Ninja.)

CAT

Yo B-Boys, Little Boy is about to tell the Ninja Story. (Screaming in the direction of the playground.)

In a matter of minutes B-Boy's from all over the Gardens made their way to the stoop of #480. Bringing with them a boom box, chips, candy, cookies, and the like. Someone in the crowd yelled "no dibbies, no snatchies." Meaning no claims and no snatching. An agreement no one honored. As they dibbied and snatched LITTLE BOY got into character. Wrapping a bandana around his afro and donning his signature shades. The story began and he instantly felt less sad. Maybe this was his happiness. His new color. Music, dancing, and storytelling. Had he found a new muse?

Was it 18 or was it the CAT that was willing to lose LITTLE BOY at the beginning of something that could have been forever.

(BLACKOUT)
(END OF SCENE)

Act 1

Scene 2

MARY JANE

SETTING:

The JFK. A recreational center built among a cluster of East Side housing projects. A safe zone. The hub of activity for the youth. A crossroads of sorts where different energies came together to form a most tenuous peace. One brokered without actual negotiation. There were B-Boys, drug dealers, gang bangers, shooters, b-ballers, the around the way girls that flocked around them all, and occasionally LITTLE BOY.

AT RISE:

LITTLE BOY enters the JFK through the basketball court. The court he loved only when he had it all to himself. The people not so much. He could do without them.

There was a small group gathered in a circle. They were the usual suspects. Amid the puffs of smoke, a strange odor emanated. Not pleasant like the smell of a pipe. But much better than that of a cigarette.

From their mouths came jokes and laughter. MURPHY was the loudest of them all. Each entrant into the park subject to the MURPHY spotlight.

B-Boy beware. No one danced their way out of that spotlight.

MURPY

What's up Little Boy? Where are you going? Don't try to walk on by like we can't see you. Come here man. I got a friend I want you to meet.

LITTLE BOY

I got a friend I want you to meet to.

MURPHY

Who?

LITTLE BOY

These.

MURPHY

These?

LITTLE BOY

These nuts. (The circle which was sky high erupted with laughter.)

MURPHY

Good one. You got me. But remember payback's a...

LITTLE BOY

A dish best served cold?

(Everyone in the circle shook their head.)

MURPHY

Come here. I want you to meet Mary Jane.

LITTLE BOY

Mary Who? I don't see no girls around you squares. Now that you mention it, I never see girls hanging with you busters. Where is this, Mary Jane?

MURPHY

Listen chump I mean champ, we get the ladies. Believe that. Right fellas?

THE CIRCLE

Like LL said the ladies love us.

MURPHY

She's right here Little Boy. (MURPHY holds up a joint.)

LITTLE BOY

That's a joint man. I don't want that. Where's this Mary Jane? I gets digits.

WOO

You don't have a phone.

(A roar of laughter erupts among them.)

MURPHY

You might get digits in math but that doesn't count. Come over here and meet her before she burns my fingers.

LITTLE BOY

You named your joint Mary Jane?

MURPHY

No Rick James named all joints Mary Jane. Check out our theme song for the summer.

(The sound of the Queen City's own Rick James belted out the lyrics to Mary Jane.)

LITTLE BOY

You turned a love song into a weed song?

MURPHY

No, Lamont you big dummy. The song is a metaphor. (MURPHY knew the word metaphor would trigger LITTLE BOY.)

LITTLE BOY

Metaphor. A figure of speech in which a word is applied to an object or action which it is not applicable.

MURPHY

Oh, damn he's gone full on Go-Go Gadget.

VANS

Full on Spock.

THE CIRCLE

Live long and prosper.

WOO (Robotic tone.)

Metaphor. A figure of speech in which a word is applied to an object. (The circle laughed even louder.)

LITTLE BOY

The words teachers use after they read your papers.

(LITTLE BOY's comment only made them laugh louder and longer.)

MURPHY

Little Boy, you need to learn how to chill. It's summertime Man. You don't have a book report to write, and you don't have a job to go to. You stay uptight. Take a hit of this Mary Jane. Let go of your worries. You walk around like you got a potato chip tucked between your butt cheeks and you're trying to walk without breaking it. You are wound tighter than the naps on the back of somebody's crush out here. I won't mention any names. (They each pointed at one other.) Don't get all paranoid like you do when we offer you a drink? It's not going to mess with your mind. Matter of fact Mary Jane is going to make you even smarter.

LITTLE BOY

Really?

MURPHY

No dummy Mary Jane won't make you smarter, but she will make you forget everything that's got you down.

LITTLE BOY

How does she do that?

MURPHY

That's a mystery.

LITTLE BOY

Another day, another mystery.

MURPHY

Yeah, something you and your little partner in crime can solve when you finish sneaking kisses.

(LITTLE BOY looked puzzled as he wondered how MURPHY knew about the kiss.)

MURPHY

Man don't worry about that. Murphy sees everything. Get this Sticky Icky.

LITTLE BOY

I thought it was Mary Jane.

MURPHY

That's what Rick James calls it. It's got lots of names. I call it Sticky Icky. You'll give it a name too. Like you do everything else. I'm going to pass this dutchie to you from the left-hand side. When you take it, it's puff, puff, give. Which means when you're done puffing it twice pass the dutchie from the left-hand side to Woo.

(MURPHY began to sing the words and the usual suspects joined him in perfect harmony.)

MURPHY

Pass the dutchie from the left-hand side. I say.

THE CIRCLE

Pass the dutchie from the left-hand side. Pass the dutchie from the left-hand side.

MURPHY

Give me the music that make me jump and prance.

WOO

My bum diggity ding ding ding bum ding bum.

LITTLE BOY

Am I supposed to ignore the pink elephant in the room?

WOO

Who are you calling a pink elephant?

LITTLE BOY

(Robotic.) Woo it's a metaphor. I'm referring to the fact that you all put your crusty lips on Mary Jane. You don't think that's gross.

MURPHY

Listen Dr. Welby, M.D. Mary Jane doesn't kill she heals. You can take the hit, or you can take a whole lotta hits.

(LITTLE BOY took the joint and paused to reflect on the scientific validity of MURPHY'S claim. Chiefly that Mary Jane would kill their nasty germs. As he pondered Mary Jane burned, and the USUAL SUSPECTS grew restless.)

WOO

Puff, puff, give. Pass the dutchie man. I put $2 dollars on this dime.

(WOO snatched the dutchie from LITTLE BOY.)

WOO

You're scared. Let me show you how it's done Little Boy. You take the dutchie. Check the fire. It's still got some burn. Put it up to your lips without slobbering on it. Inhale just enough not to choke. Hold it in deep. Then exhale slowly. (WOO executed the move.) Then repeat one more time. After that you pass the dutchie to me. I'm going to give this back to you from my right hand because you messed up the flow but kick it back to the left when you finish choking.

(WOO passed the dutchie from the right-hand side to LITTLE BOY.)

MURPHY

Oh, hell no Woo. You took a hit. When you get it back its puff give for your sneaky ass.

VANS

(Jokingly.) I want my two dollars.

A reference to the line from Better Off Dead. A cult classic among the young weed heads in the Gardens. More laughter from the circle.

LITTLE BOY

Check it. I got it. (LITTLE BOY took the dutchie from WOO and puffed just like WOO showed him.)

MURPHY

Yo you hit that son. You ain't a virgin no more. You got some big balls on you. I don't care what anybody says about the size of your balls. Mary Jane got another one. How you feel man?

LITTLE BOY

I feel mellow. Like I'm talking in slow motion. Am I talking slower?

WOO

N'all man you ain't talking slow. (WOO lied. LITTLE BOY'S speech was super slow.)

LITTLE BOY

It feels like my mouth is barely moving. Yo, I'm serious. Am I talking slower?

(At this moment they knew they had found the comic relief for the remainder of the evening.)

MURPHY

No, you're good. Does anyone think Little Boy is talking slow?

D-WILL

Sounds a little fast to me. Say something else Little Boy.

(D-WILL knew that LITTLE BOY'S literal nature would cause him to speak even slower.)

LITTLE BOY

Why – is – everyone – laughing - then?

(D-WILL'S trigger worked like a charm. They couldn't contain the laughter.)

WOO

No one's laughing. We're coughing. (Switching gears.) Little Boy, why don't you bust a move for us.

(Switching gears was the preferred strategy when dealing with a super smart yet paranoid first time weed smoker.)

LITTLE BOY

Aaight DJ Murphy let that beat drop.

(LITTLE BOY was chopped and screwed long before H-Town.)

MURPHY

Word. I got something new. I saw this on MTV a few weeks ago. Check out this Kraftwerks remix I recorded from W-U-F-O.

Murphy pressed play. Trans Europe Express flowed between Numbers and Computer Love. It was music LITTLE BOY had never heard. It took him to another place. Another galaxy. Another universe even. Somewhere far, far, away. He was less sad just like CAT said he would be. Would Mary Jane become his best friend? The sound of the music brought others who were hanging out at the JFK straight to MURPHY'S boom box and the circle of usual suspects. The circle grew into a small crowd.

The mix of different energies worked well until it didn't. It would be good if everyone knew everyone in the crowd. Every time an unfamiliar snuck into the crowd it lit the match of discord. LITTLE BOY was blazed but he would learn tonight that Mary Jane, Sticky Icky, or Dope Boy Magic as he would name it led to new moves, new moves led to attention, and attention from the wrong person led to problems. His moves tonight were on a whole new level.

QT-PIE

Little Boy, is that you? Do you remember me? I see you're real smooth with it. You're a real B-Boy.

LITTLE BOY

QT-Pie is that you? I haven't seen you since the fourth grade. What are you doing around these parts?

QT-PIE was a familiar spirit to LITTLE BOY. A blast from the past. One LITTLE BOY liked the first time he touched her little booty and got snatched up by her father.

QT-PIE

I live around the way.

LITTLE BOY

Around the way where? In the Gardens?

QT-PIE

Yeah, the building right before the plaza.

LITTLE BOY

The center entrance or the long way around by the field?

QT-PIE

By the field.

LITTLE BOY

Oh, that building. The last time I saw you your dad was holding me while you punched me in the mouth.

QT-PIE

I'm sorry about that. You were grabbing my ass and trying to kiss me. If I didn't hit you, I was going to get a whooping. It was me or you, so it had to be you. I'm going to make that up to you. I promise. I got ways to make you smile.

QT-PIE walked over and began to dance in front of LITTLE BOY. She didn't look like the nine-year-old he remembered. Her "ways" were very seductive. LITTLE BOY was feeling a certain way inside. She turned her back to him and backed up until her little bubble was touching Little Boy's little boy.

MURPHY

He's going to blow. (The crowd roared.)

LITTLE BOY

No way I'm a B-Boy. I got this.

(LITTLE BOY matched QT-PIE move for move. It was as if they had danced this dance before. Just like familiar spirits.)

MURPHY

Little Boy take it easy. You're going to explode.

LITTLE BOY

No way. We're just dancing. Catching up with a friend from the fourth grade.

WOO

This ain't the fourth grade. This the Playboy channel. I'm feeling a certain way about myself right now. Who want to have my baby tonight?

THE CROWD

NOBODY!

(Laughter erupts.)

LITTLE BOY

This ain't no Playboy channel. We got our clothes on.

QT-PIE turned to face LITTLE BOY. Their legs intertwined. She moved her hips like water. LITTLE BOY followed her lead. He was swimming in her ocean. Their parent's parents might have called it dry humping back in their day.

The groove they were in made LITTLE BOY flash a whole smile. No one in the crowd had ever seen that before. Dope Boy Magic had worked its way through his mind and freed his hands. Each hand cupped one of QT-PIE'S assets.

WOO

Little Boy got mad game? Yo Murphy fire up another joint. I gotta get my mack on tonight. Look at all these girls.

QT-PIE

Little Boy has always had game fellas. You got a girlfriend Little Boy?

LITTLE BOY

A what?

(Without answering LITTLE BOY'S question QT-PIE leaned in and slipped her tongue into his mouth. It was his first and longest French kiss of his life. The crowd thought he had given up the ghost.)

MURPHY

Damnnnnnnnnnnn.

(The kiss stopped LITTLE BOY's legs and hips from moving. He was a limp noodle.)

WOO

Yo, you killed him.

QT-PIE

He's breathing dummy. I thrill I don't kill. Somebody give me a pen.

(QT-PIE helped LITTLE BOY to the bench under the streetlight.)

MURPHY

A pen. That boy needs oxygen. He doesn't look like he's breathing to me.

(QT-PIE kissed him again and his eyes opened.)

QT PIE

He's breathing. All these "players" and no one has a pen. Is there a Mack in the crowd with a pen?

Speak of the devil and he appears. PISTOL PETE was the last person anyone wanted to see anywhere when they really needed something. His fulfillment of your needs always came with a price. He had a habit of turning something into nothing for you and nothing into everything for himself. Everyone in the neighborhood avoided him like the police or the Jehovah's Witnesses. They did so until they couldn't. He had used the music, the dancing, and the kiss as his camouflage and had gotten through the early alert systems the people had developed just for him. A one-word phrase. "SHARK!"

PISTOL PETE

I got a pen for you, QT-Pie.

QT-PIE

Can I use it?

PISTOL PETE

Only if you get it.

(Just like the devil. You had to let him in.)

MURPHY

Don't go. (Whispering.)

(QT-PIE didn't hear MURPHY. She paused and looked towards him to inquire about his comment.)

PISTOL PETE

What you say Murphy?

MURPHY

I said, "The Show."

PISTOL PETE

That's right. I am the show. I run these streets.

(PISTOL PETE pulled out his steel and pointed it towards the sky and set it off.)

PISTOL PETE

Pop. Pop. Pop.

(QT-PIE was not impressed by PISTOL PETE'S display of testosterone. She didn't know him, and she didn't heed MURPHY'S quiet warning. She walked nonchalantly over to PISTOL PETE to get his pen. There's something quite different about the energy of a lioness.)

QT-PIE

Are you done shooting your thing? Can I get the pen man?

PISTOL PETE

You can get anything you want Baby Girl.

QT-PIE

Not my name. All I need is a pen.

PISTOL PETE

That's what they all say. All I need is this, Pistol Pete. What do you need it for?

QT-PIE

I need to write something down. Ain't that obvious?

PISTOL PETE

I know you aren't giving your number to Little Boy. He's five feet tall. What can he do with you?

QT-PIE

Anything he wants. He makes me smile.

PISTOL PETE

Baby I can make you do more than smile.

MURPHY

That's not what the last girl said.

(Laughter erupts near MURPHY.)

PISTOL PETE

Murphy, I see you got jokes tonight? I can pull you right here into this light. You can have your very own comedy show. I'll pay you $100 every time you tell a joke that makes someone laugh.

MURPHY

What if they don't laugh?

PISTOL PETE

For every joke that doesn't make someone laugh I'm going to smack you across your beak.

MURPHY

With what?

PISTOL PETE

My hand stupid.

THE CIRCLE

WHEW!

MURPHY

Across my beak. I'm a bird now?

(More laughter from the crowd.)

PISTOL PETE

Yeah, a big bird.

MURPHY

Duh Dun Dunt.

(The sounds of a drum roll after a corny joke. The crowd laughed louder but PISTOL PETE did not understand the reference.)

PISTOL PETE

One more word Murphy and you're getting in this circle.

There was dead silence. Everyone present knew the deal. If they didn't laugh Murphy got slapped and if they did Murphy got $100 and they got slapped. There was at least one contemplating their level of pain tolerance.

PISTOL PETE

QT-Pie come here.

Everyone knew if she made it to PISTOL PETE her life would never be the same. He did not have the Midas touch. Everything he touched turned to coal.

D-WILL

Murphy. Music. Electric Kingdom.

Electric Kingdom flowed from the speakers. As if he had been resurrected to the land of the living LITTLE BOY rose from the bench energized. Dope Boy Magic and QT-PIE'S kiss had put him in a semi-coma. The music brought him back. The beat moved across the court and into his feet and he stood and moonwalked straight away to PISTOL PETE. This wasn't the outcome D-WILL expected. LITTLE BOY had put his head in the lion's mouth, and no one could get it out.

WOO

Bye Little Boy.

(As LITTLE BOY moonwalked past him. Silent prayers went up from the crowd.)

PISTOL PETE

Why is this fool standing here? Does he not know who I am and what I will do to him? Listen Little Boy. I'm not Ninja. This ain't that kind of story.

(Even Bad Boy's knew the story of the LITTLE BOY and the Ninja.)

LITTLE BOY

You're also not a B-Boy? So why are you standing in a B-Boy circle? You're out of pocket man. This is where B-Boy's battle.

PISTOL PETE

No, I'm not a B-Boy I'm Bad Man and I do whatever I please.

LITTLE BOY

Why are you so serious. You sound like a Mad Man.

PISTOL PETE

Murphy get your boy before he catches a fresh fade.

LITTLE BOY

Catch a fresh fade. You passed the beat back to me and I didn't see it?
Oh, you really do want to battle. Let's go. Yo Murphy.

MURPHY

What up B-Boy?

LITTLE BOY

I got a challenge. Play at Your Own Risk. (A fitting tune.)

MURPHY

Here you go.

D-WILL

Dear Lord. Please save Little Boy. He knows not what he's doing.

PISTOL PETE

Little Boy this ain't gonna end like you think.

LITTLE BOY

That's the beauty of the battle. It never does. That's why we do it. To see who's the best. Put your gun away. Let's dance.

LITTLE BOY was in rare form. His moves electric. Flowing like water. Each move a new one. Moves no one had seen before. The origin of the moves would later be attributed to the Dope Boy Magic. He inhaled one more time. If he survived the night, it would change the way B-Boy's battled forever in the Queen City. LITTLE BOY danced alone.

PISTOL PETE, like most gangsters didn't dance. What's a B-Boy battle with one B-Boy? Not much of one at all. The beat had made it to another set of feet in the circle. They weren't the feet of a B-Boy. They were the feet of the girl he had unknowingly stood up to defend. What did this mean? Could this be? Would this be? Should this be the beginning of something new? A B-Boy and a B-Girl tag teaming and battling a Grown Ass Man.

QT-PIE had made a conscious decision she would not allow LITTLE BOY to carry her torch into battle alone. He stood up when all the other lames bowed down. She was no B-Girl looking for a battle. She was an around the way girl who knew it took a neighborhood to stand up to a bully. LITTLE BOY could not do it alone. With all his boys standing around not one had his back.

Those standing around saw it happening right before their eyes. They knew they were a witness to an event. Part of a story they would tell their own children. LITTLE BOY and QT-PIE danced like their lives hung in the balance. Each looking into a mirror. For the first time seeing what others saw. They had created something new. They would call it the bridge when they told the story to their children. Not to be outdone PISTOL PETE took out his pistol and fired it into the sky. The music and the dancing came to a screeching halt.

PISTOL PETE

Little Boy did you forgot that I was still standing here? I told you I don't dance. Bad Boys throw blows and shoot shots. But you thought you could moon walk over here and disrespect me and tic-toc your way out the Thunderdome. You're so smart, you're dumb. The streets don't work like that. I don't dance but this is what I do do.

LITTLE BOY

You doo-doo'd?

(LITTLE BOY was so faded that the only thing he could do was laugh out loud. He couldn't stop if he wanted to. It was the funniest thing he had ever heard. No one knew what to do. There was one laugh then two then everyone at the same time.)

PISTOL PETE

That was a little funny. (PISTOL PETE chuckled.) I'll give you that one.

LITTLE BOY

You're not going to shoot me? I thought you said that on purpose, so you had a reason to shoot me. That was some James Bond villain shit right there. You knew it would make me laugh and that I couldn't stop.

PISTOL PETE

I'm a Bad Man just like I told you. Goldfinger.

LITTLE BOY

Just to be clear. You're not going to shoot me tonight?

PISTOL PETE

Not tonight. Someone up there likes you. But here's the deal because I'm going to write the ending to your story. Every time I see you no matter where we're at you better run until I can't... (PISTOL PETE paused.)

LITTLE BOY

Can't what?

PISTOL PETE

Little Boy.

LITTLE BOY

Yeah?

PISTOL PETE

Shark.

How did PISTOL PETE know their code word? Without saying another word PISTOL PETE pointed his pistol at LITTLE BOY's feet and pulled the trigger. No one can attest to how fast LITTLE BOY ran because everyone took off running at the same time. Each in their own direction.

Just like that. Another chapter had been added to the legend of LITTLE BOY. In one evening, he had lost his virginity to Mary Jane, kissed in

France, danced in an ocean, went into a coma, took it to the Bridge, battled a BAD MAN, and ran faster than a speeding bullet.

As LITTLE BOY turned the corner towards his house, he heard a special request coming from Dwayne's radio on the first floor of #480.

DISC JOCKEY

Listen up Queen City we got a special request going out to the Gardens to a B-Boy from his around way girl. She's leaving the red light on tonight. Call her as soon as you get home. I heard she's just like the next song. Cutie Pie on the Quiet Storm. You better call that girl Little Boy. She's waiting.

(Cutie Pie blazed across the airwaves and out the window.)

LITTLE BOY

QT-Pie you're the reason why. I love you so I don't want you to go.

(LITTLE BOY had made it home again after another epic battle. He definitely had friends in high places.)

(BLACKOUT)
(END OF SCENE)

Act 1

Scene 3

SUNSHINE AND RAINDROPS

SETTING: The Queen City. The East Side. A hop and skip and a jump away from downtown.

AT RISE: LITTLE BOY is sitting on the porch as are many on the block. It was Saturday morning, and the weather was perfect. A beautiful day. Birds singing. Children playing.

MR. HOPPER stood looking admiring his new beauty. SETTIE walked out the front door and took her seat on the porch. She was the first girl LITTLE BOY had met in the QUEEN CITY.

SETTIE

Hey Little Boy.

LITTLE BOY

Hey Settie.

SETTIE

What are you doing?

LITTLE BOY

Reading.

SETTIE

You're always reading. Is that a new book?

MR. HOPPER

Settie stop all that yelling across the street. Go on over there but stay where I can see you.

SETTIE

Oh Grandpa. We were just talking.

MR. HOPPER

You were talking too loud. I can't hear myself think with all that racket.

MOTHER HOPPER

Earl you ought to leave them kids alone and come up on this porch and spend some time with your wife. Settie go on across the street to Momma Howell's before I have to bop your grandfather in the head.

SETTIE

OK Grandma. I have to get my bag of penny candy from my room.

(SETTIE went inside the house to get her bag of penny candy.)

MR. HOPPER

This weather is perfect.

MOTHER HOPPER

Yes, it is Earl. Praise the LORD.

MR. HOPPER

I'll praise him when I can go down to the pier with my fishing pole.

MOTHER HOPPER

You better hush before you get hit with a lightning bolt. You ain't going to praise the LORD until you can go fishing? While you over there talking about fishing you should be on a ladder painting this house like you promised me two years ago.

MR. HOPPER

Woman you know about my back.

MOTHER HOPPER

Yes, I do. That's why you aren't fishing mister.

MR. HOPPER

There you go with your photographic memory. Why doesn't it work when I need it to?

MOTHER HOPPER

Like when Mr. Hopper?

MR. HOPPER

Like when I'm looking for the keys to my car, or when I can't find my hat or how about when my glasses grow legs and walk away from my own nightstand. You and your granddaughter both know I can't put anything down in this house without one of you swooping in like a hawk and moving it. Then no one knows anything when they see me looking for my stuff. Does any of that ring a bell?

MOTHER HOPPER

Earl I am not fooling with you today. No one touches your stuff.

(SETTIE entered the porch through the front door.)

MR. HOPPER

Settie we're not going to be running in and out of this house all day long. Why can't you get everything you need the first time?

SETTIE

I don't know.

MR. HOPPER

You hear that. She don't know. You better not eat all that candy. You know we don't do cavities in this house.

SETTIE

Grandpa, I brush my teeth three times a day just like you told me. Don't I have the pearliest pearlies?

(SETTIE flashed her signature million-dollar smile.)

MOTHER HOPPER

Girl, your smile reminds me of my momma. Every time you smile, I think of heaven.

MR. HOPPER

Heaven?

MOTHER HOPPER

Earl look at that smile. Bright enough to light up the world.

MR. HOPPER

It should be we spent a fortune on it. Every time I see it, all I can think of is the poor house. Now gone across the street before a car comes and tell Little Boy I got my eyes on him.

MOTHER HOPPER

Settie don't tell Little Boy that. We're not going to let your grandfather give him a complex. The boy came here in the middle of the night knowing no one in the city. Bless his heart. He's a nice boy.

SETTIE

I won't Grandma. I'll be back later.

MOTHER HOPPER

Make sure you look both ways.

(SETTIE looked both ways just like MOTHER HOPPER told her and when the street was clear she ran across to MOMMA HOWELL'S house.)

MR. HOPPER

Baby I don't care what anybody says. That little boy got a lot of sneakiness in him.

MOTHER HOPPER

You know they say you can see a lot of yourself in others.

MR. HOPPER

I don't know who "they" are, but I know "they" are wrong. We are nothing alike. I was nine years old once and I wasn't that strange. All he does is read, and he never looks at you when he speaks to you. I don't trust anybody that can't look you in the eyes.

MOTHER HOPPER

Earl I'm going to get you something to cool you off because you're in rare form today.

(MOTHER HOPPER walked into the house to get MR. HOPPER a glass of iced tea.)

SETTIE

Little Boy you're always in those books. What are you reading this time?

LITTLE BOY

I have a routine. I start every Saturday with the paper because I want to know what's going on around me. Then I read a new book. My favorites are westerns. This is the new Louie Lamour book. He's my favorite author.

SETTIE

Really? A city boy that likes cowboys.

LITTLE BOY

I'm actually a country boy who happens to be stuck in the city.

SETTIE

That is true. I bet you want a horse too.

LITTLE BOY

I do. I think every boy should have a horse.

SETTIE

On all this concrete? If you had one where would put it? What would you name it?

LITTLE BOY

If I had one, I'd ride it back home to Georgia. I would name it Lightening. That's how fast I would ride out of here. What would you name yours?

SETTIE

I never thought about owning a horse but if I had one to ride, I'd ride with you and I'd name it Brownie.

LITTLE BOY

Stop playing.

SETTIE

I'm for real. I would name it after you because you have the prettiest big brown eyes I've ever seen, and you gave me the idea. You always make me think about things I never thought about.

LITTLE BOY

That's a plot twist.

SETTIE

Little Boy I've known you four years and I don't know your last name. What is it?

LITTLE BOY

Blue.

SETTIE

Blue. Little Boy Blue. I love that name. I can just see a Little Boy Blue Jr. with a rocking horse named Lightning. Doesn't that sound cute?

LITTLE BOY

I would never do that.

SETTIE

Have a little boy with a rocking horse?

LITTLE BOY

No, name him after me.

SETTIE

Why not? Imagine him in his little vest and his little leather pants or whatever you call those things.

LITTLE BOY

You mean chaps.

SETTIE

Yes chaps. We can't forget about the silver spurs and cowboy boots and the belt with the giant buckle. We could dress him up so cute.

LITTLE BOY

You mean you could dress him so cute.

SETTIE

Can't you see him spinning his little pistols and talking all tough like the cowboys do? Spitting his tobacco, walking in the saloon, and moseying on up to the bar. Smacking the bartender in the face just to show everyone in the saloon he means business.

LITTLE BOY

Why would he do all that?

SETTIE

Because he's edgy like his father.

LITTLE BOY

Edgy?

SETTIE

You're quiet but always thinking. It's impossible to tell what's going on behind those big, beautiful brown eyes of yours.

(SETTIE had a way of making LITTLE BOY feel flushed.)

LITTLE BOY

Stop it.

SETTIE

One day I'm going to write the story of Little Boy Blue. The cowboy who rode through the Queen City on a horse and tamed this concrete jungle.

LITTLE BOY

A cowboy and a horse in a jungle?

SETTIE

You like it too?

LITTLE BOY

Yeah, but I'm the only one strong enough to carry this name.

SETTTIE

That's a little edgy. You wouldn't share it with your son?

LITTLE BOY

I wouldn't call that glory. This name isn't easy to carry. I've had to fight over it. I would save my little boy from all that.

SETTIE

You do see a son in your future.

LITTLE BOY

I can't see past eighteen.

SETTIE

What? Why eighteen?

LITTLE BOY

It's a long story. I'll tell you one day.

(Translation. None of your business. You'll never know. Don't ever ask again. It was the hidden language of LITTLE BOY and very few spoke it.)

SETTIE

OK. I'll be waiting. I'm so glad you moved here, Little Boy.

LITTLE BOY

I wouldn't call it moved here, but why are you glad?

SETTIE

Because you're unique. You're not like anyone around here.

LITTLE BOY

I'm not from around here.

SETTIE

That's the point. I think it's the way you think. You make me think. I like that.

(LITTLE BOY smiled his signature half smile.)

SETTIE

I'm going to change that thing you do with your face.

LITTLE BOY

What thing?

SETTIE

When your mind fights your heart. I can tell that your heart wants to smile but your mind fights it so hard that I can see the fight taking place right on your face.

(SETTIE showed LITTLE BOY his signature half smile. It was the first time he had seen it from another.)

LITTLE BOY

I don't know what you're talking about.

(LITTLE BOY had lied. He knew exactly what SETTIE was talking about. It only added to his sadness. He thought he had hidden it from the world.)

SETTIE

You do Little Boy.

(SETTIE walked over and sat in the chair with LITTLE BOY.)

SETTIE

I'm going to make you smile. I like you and I know you like me. You're such a mystery. Easy to talk to yet a boy of few words.

LITTLE BOY

I feel a but coming.

SETTIE

The more I talk to you the more I want to know about you. But you got this way of saying only what you're going to say and nothing more.

LITTLE BOY

And there it is. People say that a lot about me. I wish it were different. I really do. I wish I didn't feel what I feel. I wish I knew more. I wish I had more to talk about. I have figured everything out by myself. I'm ten. What do I know about the world? My life is a month of raindrops. I like you too, Settie.

SETTIE

I can tell that something happened to you. You may never want to tell me. Whatever it is you didn't do anything to deserve it. Remember this Little

Boy. Life is like a rainbow. No matter how bad it gets its always up there. A reminder that the storm will pass.

LITTLE BOY

I like listening to you talk. You talk like an old lady, and you talk enough for both of us. In a clever way. Not annoyingly like a chatterbox. Your words calm me down and you don't get upset when I have nothing to say. Another thing. You're always happy. I thought something was wrong with you at first. Because who is happy all the time?

SETTIE

Wow. I am. That was a lot from you. We're making progress today. Hey, look, the Tamale man is coming.

LITTLE BOY

I see him but I don't have any money.

SETTIE

Don't worry about it. I'll buy you one.

MR. HOPPER

Settie Brielle Hopper there's more than one chair on that porch.

SETTIE

Hey grandpa. We're talking about tamales.

MR. HOPPER

I bet Little Boy was talking about tamales. He looks like he's starving to death.

(MR. HOPPER pointed his fingers at his eyes and then his index finger at LITTLE BOY.)

MOTHER HOPPER

Earl, I see two little kids sitting in a chair talking and laughing. Let's face it, you're going to be uncomfortable with Settie liking anyone. You know she's going to grow up right?

(MR. HOPPER remained silent. It was a rhetorical question. He looked on as the TAMALE MAN made his way down the street.)

TAMALE MAN

Hot tamales. Get your hot tamales. Always fresh. You know I got the best. Get them while they're hot. Cause I got a lot. Hot tamales. Peanuts. Come and get your peanuts. Fresh and hot. Right out the pot.

A child from down the street screamed TAMALE MAN and children came from everywhere. LITTLE BOY and SETTIE ran down the stairs from the porch to meet the TAMALE MAN. She held his hand as they ran down the stairs. LITTLE BOY smiled and MR. HOPPER noticed. He had never seen LITTLE BOY smile.

As LITTLE BOY and SETTIE approached the TAMALE MAN, MR. JIMMIE, he came staggering around the corner. His energy was different today. Something was off. He wasn't the usual jokester. He didn't have his balloons. MR. JIMMIE made the most amazing balloon animals. It was the one thing he could do that made people see him as human. Just like that the day had changed. There would be raindrops. So much for sunshine and rainbows.

MR. JIMMIE

Hey little ones, can you loan me a dollar so I can get me a tamale? I'll pay you back tomorrow after my balloon show.

MR. HOPPER

Mr. Jimmie, go about your business and leave those kids alone.

MOTHER HOPPER

Earl, you know Mr. Jimmie don't mean those kids no harm. You know they messed that boy's head up over there in Korea. He has never been the same. They didn't give that boy any help when they brought him back home. He didn't do that to himself.

MR. HOPPER

I know that Baby, but I don't want anyone watching thinking they can get that close to my baby girl, and I don't want Settie thinking it's OK for her to get that close to any man.

MOTHER HOPPER

I understand.

MOMMA HOWELL heard the commotion and walked out onto her porch. She had watched over MR. JIMMIE for more than twenty years since he returned from the war. Shellshocked is how they classified him. Abandoned is what they did to him. MOMMA HOWELL knew that every time she saw him it was a miracle. MR. JIMMIE taught her more about faith than anything in this world.

MOMMA HOWELL

Mr. Jimmie, come on over here, I got some money for you. Don't ever ask children for money. You know better than that.

MR. JIMMIE looked up to locate MOMMA HOWELL. He was somewhere between the Queen City and Korea. He heard her voice, and he heard the curses from soldiers all around him. Before he could find MOMMA HOWELL, a squad car came screeching to a halt and two of the Queen Cities boys in blue jumped out and ran towards MR. JIMMIE.

OFFICER BILLIE

Jimmie, I need you to get away from those kids because we need to talk.

MR. JIMMIE

What do we need to talk about? Don't you see what's going here? These boys been chasing me all day. My own people trying to hurt me. I'm not messing with nobody. I'm trying to help. You need to stop messing with me and start dealing with them. Y'all always picking on us. We're supposed to be on the same side. I'm tired of this.

(MR. JIMMIE turned towards the officer.)

MOMMA HOWELL

Officers, what's going on? Y'all need to calm down. You're going to get him upset. We all know Jimmie wouldn't hurt a fly. If you get him going you won't be able to turn him off.

OFFICER BILLIE

Ma'am, we have a report from a little girl's father two blocks away. We're here to take Jimmie in and ask him some questions. He can come the easy way or the hard way. But he's coming with us. We can't leave him on the street. If that Little Girl's father and his friends catch him, we can't protect him. All we heard was that there was a balloon trick that didn't go right, and no one will say what that really means.

MOMMA HOWELL

Well let me talk to him.

OFFICER BILLIE

I would if I could. We're dealing with a pretty serious allegation. This is official police business right now. For your protection and ours I need you on the sidewalk.

(MR. JIMMIE recognized MOMMA HOWELL through the fog of war and when he saw OFFICER BILLIE put his hand on her shoulder to move her to the sidewalk. That was all it took. He was triggered.)

MR. JIMMIE

Get your hands off Big Momma.

MR. JIMMIE had moved faster than anyone realized he could. He grabbed the arm of OFFICER BILLIE and snatched him away from BIG MOMMA. The speed and strength surprised everyone. OFFICER BILLIE went flying one way and his whistle the other. His partner made the call for backup and jumped out the squad car with his club drawn. He came in with force, striking MR. JIMMIE, who couldn't go down. He was back in Korea. Surrounded by boys in the same uniform he was wearing. Beating him for being himself.

The backups arrived in two cars. They jumped out and joined the frenzy. If one was going down, they were all going down. Such was the code. They struck MR. JIMMIE repeatedly.

LITTLE BOY counted seventy-seven raindrops. Each strike a raindrop. Each raindrop a tear. The sound of the sticks hitting MR. JIMMIE'S arms, legs, torso, and skull, transformed his roar into a scream, then a whimper, and finally there was nothing but silence.

SETTIE, MOMMA HOWELL, MR. HOPPER, MOTHER HOPPER and the others in the crowd were screaming so loud for the officers to stop, that no one noticed LITTLE BOY sitting in the middle of the street screaming in silence. His tears hit the pavement like thunder.

LITTLE BOY sat up in bed and screamed STOP! His hand and finger extended. Heart racing. Breathing accelerated. He realized he was home. It was a nightmare. Would it ever end? He sobbed silently. It would never be over. Life had never been the same. How could it be? That was the last time he ever saw MR. JIMMIE.

(BLACKOUT)
(END OF SCENE)
(END OF ACT)

Act 2

Scene 1

INVINCIBLE

SETTING: The School of Honor. The shining light on the side of the hill. A melting pot or a tea kettle. It all depended on the hypothesis that governed the experiment.

AT RISE: LITTLE BOY approaches the senior lounge. The cave where seniors congregate during study halls or the unexcused absence from a meaningless class.

Today was the latter. It was the act of skipping. A skill LITTLE BOY had perfected. After years of being absent with cause, his return to the bubble made being present and absent at the same time a reality. An act that fit LITTLE BOY to the tee.

PABLO
What's going on Bro? I see you made it to school today.

LITTLE BOY
I see you working on your Tonight Show jokes. Nothing going on here.

PABLO

You must be skipping?

LITTLE BOY

Yeah. You know the routine.

PABLO

Who you got this period?

LITTLE BOY

We're in the same class man.

PABLO

Oh yeah that's right. Don't act like you come to school. You've missed more school than anyone I've ever known.

LITTLE BOY

I'm a country boy living in a cold, cold, world. I don't belong here. I'm a prisoner of war. I don't know how y'all deal with this cold. It's torture.

PABLO

I seem to remember a certain country boy going back to the south and running right back to this cold with his tail between his legs. Now what could make you run back to this snow? That's the million-dollar question that you have never answered. Care to shed some light on that Sir?

LITTLE BOY

What can I say? I missed you.

PABLO

Stop lying. You don't like people. What's your excuse for skipping? You didn't do the homework?

LITTLE BOY

I'm not working at home. Power to the people.

PABLO

What does that have to do with homework?

LITTLE BOY

Everything. I'm done writing about people that don't interest me.

PABLO

I thought you loved writing.

LITTLE BOY

I like to create. When was the last time we did something creative in this joint? This place is like a prison. I'm not in the mood for Chuckie today.

PABLO

I thought that was your boy. He's always calling your name.

LITTLE BOY

Do I ever say anything? He said he doesn't appreciate my level of engagement.

PABLO

Engagement? What did he mean by that?

LITTLE BOY

I didn't know what it meant either. He didn't explain it. He said I had all the potential in the world but didn't give a damn.

PABLO

What made him say that?

LITTLE BOY

My PSAT scores. My nomination to Who's Who in American High School Students. The fact that I do just enough to not get kicked out.

PABLO

You scored that high? You got into that?

LITTLE BOY

I did.

PABLO

You didn't tell your boys.

LITTLE BOY

Nope. That means something to the school. It doesn't mean anything to me.

PABLO

It means something to us. People that look like you and me. (Pointing to his skin.)

LITTLE BOY

What can I do with it? I can't afford the book my name is written in. There are people here with the same skin color who look at me with more scorn than those whose skin is not like mine.

PABLO

It still means something. They know who you are.

LITTLE BOY

I don't even know who I am. What could they know about me? How I fit on a graph? Where I fall on a curve? It doesn't change anything for me. I'm only doing what I must to get out of here. Call it my own private civil disobedience. Nothing here is what it seems.

PABLO

Somebody sounds a little frustrated. I know we've been here a long time. I know we see the same people day after day, year after year. That gets old. It might even feel like a prison. But it's not a prison and you know it.

LITTLE BOY

You think? It might not rise to the level of prison. But there is something about it that isn't right. I can't put a finger on it. But I know this isn't good for us.

PABLO

Speak on it. Free your mind and let your conscience swing.

LITTLE BOY

In the beginning I really bought into this joint. Like it was modern-day Camelot, and we were the young knights of the roundtable. A place where the best and the brightest walked the halls. I tried to be that. I really put in the effort. Burning the midnight oil even while I was sick. No matter how hard I tried I couldn't win the race. I couldn't even place. That really depressed me.

PABLO

I never looked at it like that.

LITTLE BOY

Learning was the only thing that kept me sane in this city. I thought the reason I couldn't reach the top was because everyone above me was better than me. It didn't help that they were all white. That added another layer of depression to it.

PABLO

You're making me think.

LITTLE BOY

Danger Will Robinson. Then one day I walked in the lounge and saw the Penny Loafer mafia holding the carbon of a test they had stolen from the printing office outside the teachers' lounge. They were cheating the whole time. Call me naïve but I never imagined students would cheat here. No one thought about cheating at our neighborhood schools. We were happy to have teachers that gave a damn about us.

PABLO

Damn you right man. What did you do?

LITTLE BOY

Nothing. I just stood there looking at them. I was in shock.

PABLO

Why didn't you say something?

LITTLE BOY

To whom? Them? What was I supposed to do? Go to the office and make a public announcement? Better yet, what if I had made a citizen's arrest of the Queen Cities elite?

PABLO

You could have done something.

LITTLE BOY

Like what? Go Bass Reeves on them?

PABLO

Who the hell is Bass Reeves?

LITTLE BOY

The real Lone Ranger. Another story for another day. You think life is fair? Do you remember the blind substitute with the dog last year?

PABLO

Yeah, he came in for one day and gave a long ass loyalty speech and then a quiz.

LITTLE BOY

Exactly and what did everyone do right after he appealed to their sense of honor and asked them not take advantage of his disability?

PABLO

Pulled out their books and notes.

LITTLE BOY

That's called cheating. Why would he ask us not to cheat? I didn't connect the dots then because it was just a quiz. They play games with us here.

PABLO

You know I'm a conspiracy theorist. What if that was an experiment? A psychological operation pulled on kids.

LITTLE BOY

What if he wasn't blind?

PABLO

Exactly. Sitting there looking at us laughing behind those fake glasses. With his fake ass seeing eye dog. Mr. Charlie is always up to no good.

LITTLE BOY

What is cheating inside an experiment? Is it a form of protest? Sticking it to the man?

PABLO

I can't do philosophy right now. Cheating is cheating. I don't care if you're cheating to get ahead or cheating as a protest. You are making me think too much today. I skipped this period because I didn't want to think.

LITTLE BOY

Look at us. Why are we skipping? We used to love learning. We aren't happy here. We haven't been happy for a while.

PABLO

Gotham's finest seem to be happy when they skip. They don't seem to have a care in the world. They have GPA's above four. What does that even mean?

LITTLE BOY

They have all the answers to all the tests. Do you think everyone cheats?

PABLO

I don't know about everyone. I have never heard of anyone getting caught here. Why is that? We have security.

LITTLE BOY

Security is a joke. There are more drugs in this school than a pharmacy. Do you think everyone that looks like us cheats?

PABLO

Who knows? Why don't you ask Ebony what she thinks?

LITTLE BOY

Ebony, I got a couple of questions for you.

EBONY

What do you want to know Little Boy? Are we an item this year? Sure. Why not? Are we going to break up at the end of the year? You already know it's a yes. You know the routine. Is that it? Did I answer your questions?

LITTLE BOY

No. But thanks for the clarity. Here are the real questions. Do you think everyone cheats? Do you think some do it better than others?

EBONY

In relationships? Yes.

LITTLE BOY

No. I'm talking about academics.

EBONY

You weren't clear on the matter. Which is really important. It's a loaded question. To clarify. Do I think you, Pablo, and everyone I know at this school, cheats? The answer to that is yes.

LITTLE BOY

Really?

PABLO

I didn't see that coming.

EBONY

Your second question. Are some cheaters better at cheating than other cheaters? Of course. We're not equal. If it can be done there will be those who can do it better than others. Duh. That's common sense.

PABLO

Debate club paid off. Go head girl. There is a real place for you at City Hall. Now for the million-dollar question and the win. Do you remember the blind substitute from last year?

EBONY

I do. There was something weird about him and his dog.

PABLO

My thoughts exactly. Like the dog was blind and he could see.

LITTLE BOY

That's exactly what I thought but couldn't put it in words.

PABLO

Ebony did you cheat?

EBONY

Pablo, why are you trying to make me incriminate myself? I can only say I saw a lot of open books and open notes.

LITTLE BOY

Did you see or notice an open book or notes on your own desk?

PABLO

You got her squirming now Little Boy.

EBONY

Trust me, he does not, and I do not recall.

PABLO

With a straight face even.

LITTLE BOY

Not sure what that was about. I'm going to keep it moving. I'll make it easy for everyone. Let's run with the assumption that everyone has the potential to cheat. What would make one cheater better than another?

PABLO

Are we talking strictly academics?

LITTLE BOY

Yes Geraldo Rivera.

PABLO

I would say intelligence.

LITTLE BOY

What say you, Ebony?

EBONY

I think it's information.

LITTLE BOY

Elaborate.

PABLO

You didn't ask me to elaborate.

LITTLE BOY

Chill Pablo.

EBONY

Let's say you're standing before a table. There is box with the questions, a box with the answers, and a box with the questions and the answers.

LITTLE BOY

I like this. Keep going.

EBONY

Finally.

LITTLE BOY

A paper cut. But OK. Keep going.

LILLY

You know I was eavesdropping. I couldn't stay out of this discussion any longer. You need more than information.

(EBONY rolls her eyes.)

LITTLE BOY

Do you think its intelligence?

LILLY

Define intelligence.

LITTLE BOY

Intelligence. The ability to learn or understand or to deal with new or trying situations or the ability to apply knowledge to manipulate one's environment or to think abstractly as measured by objective criteria.

PABLO

Easy Webster. You know I only talk jive.

LITTLE BOY

I know Mr. Jefferson. Do they print in jive on your tests?

PABLO

No but I wish they would.

LITTLE BOY

Maybe it's a mix of intelligence and information. I move to table this segment for later. Can we address the real elephant in the room?

(They looked around the senior lounge.)

EBONY

What is that Little Boy?

LITTLE BOY

Why isn't there anyone that looks like us in the top ten? Weren't we the best of the best in our neighborhood schools?

LILLIE

Touché. I know I was.

EBONY

You were?

PABLO

Uh oh. Cat fight.

LITTLE BOY

So, what happened to us when we got here? Did we run into people who were so much smarter than us or is there something else going on? Are we fighting with one arm behind our back?

PABLO

We've been here six, seven, and eight years. All the melting should have taken place by now. If they were that advanced, we would have learned things and changed the way we did things.

LITTLE BOY

I don't feel melted at all. What did we get from getting stirred in this pot? Can you gain and lose something at the same time? Here's what I've learned. Nothing here is what it seems. But as painful as that may seem it brought everything Pops told me into focus.

PABLO

I didn't know you knew Willie Stargell.

LITTLE BOY

I don't. Pop's is my brother's father. He told me there are two tracks. One built with best there is to offer and the other made from the least they can find. Neither runner knows there's a difference between the tracks because they never see the other track. They each assume they're running on the same track.

LILLY

So, the runner who learned how to sneak into the teachers' lounge and steal the test thinks that all runners do so.

EBONY

Or do they think that runners who have a natural fear of authority would never think of such a thing or conceive that anyone else would either?

LITTLE BOY

Eureka.

PABLO

Eureka. Man, you have been here too long.

LITTLE BOY

Yes, I have. I've carried this feeling for seven years that they were on a level that I could never reach. I started to believe there was something wrong with me.

PABLO

All this time and we have never spoken about this. Does anyone else feel this way?

EBONY

We have all felt something. It's impossible not to. It's like looking at the pictures of presidents and thinking that with all the brilliant Black men that have walked this Earth not one was capable of being president of a country this lost.

PABLO

And the fine, I meant brilliant Black women.

LITTLE BOY

Much respect to the ladies. What if that was the intent of the whole experiment? To make us feel like we weren't good enough. Feel like we were failures and carry that feeling back home.

PABLO

That's heavy.

LITTLE BOY

I know. I need a joint. I remember the feeling of pride I had when I was accepted here. Like I had made it. I had arrived, won the lottery even. I had been labeled young black and gifted for years. I didn't know I would leave all my friends behind to come here to feel like this.

PABLO

Do you think the teachers knew?

LITTLE BOY

They had to. They build plans on top of plans. Did they run just one experiment?

LILLY

There had to be at least two experiments, each with their own hypothesis, run on our people. What happens to the neighborhood schools when they remove the young, black, and gifted and what happens to the young, black, and gifted when they are mixed with others?

LITTLE BOY

Now we're getting somewhere. Each one of us is a data point in someone's quantitative analysis. The reason someone has the letters PhD behind their name right now. A discussion behind closed doors. A conversation they will never have with us because they can't.

PABLO

You're right. If they asked questions like that, we would have realized we were part of an experiment a long time ago.

EBONY

I think you're right Little Boy.

LITTLE BOY

You do?

EBONY

I do.

PABLO

And now I pronounce you husband and wife.

LILLY

Pablo, you are so stupid.

LITTLE BOY

Spot on Lilly. It might be too late to make a difference for us. But it could be effective for those who come through those doors after us.

PABLO

You're right Man. We're at the end of the road. What do we want to leave behind, a stupid brick with our name in it?

LITTLE BOY

I want to share our truth with those who come behind us. I want to prepare and protect their minds.

EBONY

That's going to be hard. There's no unity among us. We came here and split into these cliques. I feel like we lost something trying to fit in. You could call it many things. But too me it all boils down to love. If we find our love of self. We will find us. If we find us, we're going to make a way for our future. We can still leave a legacy here that lasts forever. If you ask me that would be the greatest thing that came out of this unspoken experiment.

LITTLE BOY

You hit the nail on the head Ebony. Pablo, Do you think we can find this love?

PABLO

We found each other, didn't we?

EBONY

We did. They may have brought us here. But we found each other.

LITTLE BOY

Time is flying. We're all going in different directions. We may never see each other again. We must seize this moment. This is something no one can take away from us.

LILLY

You're right. They may have run this experiment and they may have collected tons of data that we may never be privy too. But I bet you they never saw this coming. They don't own our story. We're going to tell it. Believe that.

LITTLE BOY picked up his guitar and began to play the first notes of what would become their story. Four friends from four different corners of the city who had known each other for years had finally found their love. They stood up and formed a circle.

LITTLE BOY

When we find love, we'll find us.

EBONY

When we find us, we'll find love.

LITTLE BOY & PABLO

When we find love, we'll find us.

EBONY & LILLIE

When we find us, we'll find love.

LITTLE BOY

I hate this place Ebony but I'm glad I found you.

EBONY

I know you're glad you found me. (With a wink.)

LITTLE BOY

I thought we'd dance this dance forever.

EBONY

So, did I.

LITTLE BOY

I'll see you on the other side.

(LITTLE BOY grabbed EBONY, kissed her, and ducked out of the lounge.)

(BLACKOUT)
(END OF SCENE)

Act 2

Scene 2

3 PAIR OF PANTS & 3 SHIRTS

SETTING: The Mall in Eastern Hills.

AT RISE: LITTLE BOY is sitting on a bench in the middle of
                    the mall. He had taken three buses, used one fare
                    and two transfers during the winter to arrive at this
                    moment. The midpoint of the year.

                    The moment when the wardrobe for the remain-
                    der of the year was purchased. Marrying the
                    first half ensemble with the second. Completing
                    the arrangement of the less fortunate. It was an
                    annual ritual.

                    OLD EARTH sits down next to LITTLE BOY.

OLD EARTH

Long day?

LITTLE BOY

Long life.

OLD EARTH

You're too young to be that tired.

LITTLE BOY

I don't feel young.

OLD EARTH

You grew up too fast.

LITTLE BOY

What does that mean?

OLD EARTH

Your trials began early. You've been tested.

LITTLE BOY

You could say that.

OLD EARTH

But you're still standing.

LITTLE BOY

Barely.

OLD EARTH

Barely is sufficient. Ask the man in the wheelchair.

LITTLE BOY

I suppose.

OLD EARTH

There are many ways to look at a situation.

LITTLE BOY

I can only see what I can.

OLD EARTH

Most can't see at all. I think you see much more than you think.

LITTLE BOY

How do you know that? What do you see?

OLD EARTH

Old eyes.

LITTLE BOY

Old eyes?

OLD EARTH

We used to call them two-way mirrors a long time ago.

LITTLE BOY

You can see both ways?

OLD EARTH

I can and so can you.

LITTLE BOY

I wish I didn't.

OLD EARTH

No, you don't. You can feel everything. It's one of your superpowers. Most can't feel anything. You feel what they can't.

(LITTLE BOY giggled nervously. He wasn't sure why and didn't know if it was appropriate.)

LITTLE BOY

I've never been on the other side of this.

OLD EARTH

Being watched? You're used to blending in like wallpaper and looking through those mirrors at everyone else.

LITTLE BOY

I do that a lot.

OLD EARTH

We do that a lot. Your life has meaning and a purpose.

LITTLE BOY

No one knows I exist.

OLD EARTH

I know you exist. Do you know you exist? You can change things later with the others.

LITTLE BOY

How?

OLD EARTH

Blaze a trail so bright that they can't miss you.

LITTLE BOY

All they see is a poor boy from the projects who doesn't know his father.

OLD EARTH

Is that what you see? Would you be different if you came from the suburbs?

LITTLE BOY

I don't know. Maybe.

OLD EARTH

You know. You wouldn't. Comfort wouldn't change your plight. You once lived in the suburbs. What's on your mind right now?

LITTLE BOY

I did when I was little, but I'm still tired of being poor.

OLD EARTH

If you were rich, you'd be tired of that too.

LITTLE BOY

You think so?

OLD EARTH

I know so. Most rich people grow tired of its meaninglessness after a couple of years, and they fall off into drugs and alcohol and the sort. Why are you tired of being poor?

LITTLE BOY

I can't escape it.

OLD EARTH

Stop trying. It's an experience. Are you poor?

LITTLE BOY

Look at me.

OLD EARTH

What do you want me to look at? You or your clothes?

LITTLE BOY

You can't see me without my clothes.

OLD EARTH

I beg to differ. I see you better than you see yourself and I can't see a thing.

LITTLE BOY

Wait. What do you mean?

OLD EARTH

I'm a man of simple words. The obvious is the obvious. I'm letting you paint a picture in my mind with your words.

(OLD EARTH took off his dark shades and looked in the direction of LITTLE BOY. LITTLE BOY looked into the cosmos of OLD EARTH'S MIRRORS.)

LITTLE BOY

You couldn't see me until you heard me?

OLD EARTH

I felt your presence.

LITTLE BOY

I see.

OLD EARTH

Oh, now you can see. Interesting. You have to talk more. You have a story to tell. A story that doesn't belong to you. It belongs to the world. A gift that was given to you from on high. You have chosen this path of indifference. Showing up like a blank page in a coloring book. Letting other folks color your page with their words and getting angry when they make you whatever they want you to be.

LITTLE BOY

I see.

OLD EARTH

You say that a lot.

LITTLE BOY

So, I'm not poor?

OLD EARTH

Oh, you're poor. Even I can see that.

LITTLE BOY

Wait a minute. I thought you said you only saw my words.

OLD EARTH

I said I saw the image you were painting with your words. It was pretty poor. Did you lie?

LITTLE BOY

No. I'm confused now.

OLD EARTH

You do that a lot too.

LITTLE BOY

What?

OLD EARTH

Give up or run away when life throws you a curve you can't hit or won't hit.

LITTLE BOY

I'm still sitting here.

OLD EARTH

Are you sure about that?

LITTLE BOY

Yes, I'm sitting right next to you.

OLD EARTH

Your body is here. That is a fact. But your mind left as soon as the question became uncomfortable.

LITTLE BOY

My friends say I do that a lot.

OLD EARTH

I see why.

LITTLE BOY

What does that mean?

OLD EARTH

When you find yourself in a situation that you can't escape from you find a way to disappear inside yourself.

LITTLE BOY

I do that a lot.

It's obvious. It's self-preservation. A low-level defense mechanism.

LITTLE BOY

Oh, that's what I was doing.

OLD EARTH

Yes. It's something you taught yourself.

LITTLE BOY

How would I know how to do that?

OLD EARTH

We are all given gifts.

LITTLE BOY

How do I change things?

OLD EARTH

Use your gift. I gave you the key.

LITTLE BOY

My words.

OLD EARTH

Yes, use your words.

LITTLE BOY

Tell my story.

OLD EARTH

To the world or others will.

(LITTLE BOY closed his eyes a second to ponder and OLD EARTH departed the area as if he had disappeared into thin air. His mission for today accomplished.)

LITTLE BOY

I should share them with the... Hey. Where'd you go?

(LITTLE BOY stood up and looked around the mall for OLD EARTH as LITTLE MOMMA approached him.)

LITTLE MOMMA

Who are you talking to?

LITTLE BOY

There was this old blind man sitting right here. We were talking. I swear to you. He was sitting right next to me.

LITTLE MOMMA

And he just up and left you standing here in the middle of the mall talking to yourself?

LITTLE BOY

He asked me a question. I closed my eyes to think, and then he was gone.

LITTLE MOMMA

What did I tell you about closing your eyes around people?

LITTLE BOY

You said don't do it.

LITTLE MOMMA

Why?

LITTLE BOY

Because I can't see what's going on around me.

LITTLE MOMMA

And?

LITTLE BOY

Someone's going to split my wig.

LITTLE MOMMA

Your words not mine, but you got the gist of the message.

LITTLE BOY

I'll try to remember.

LITTLE MOMMA

Don't try to remember. Stop doing it. What if I slapped you every time you did it? Would you still forget?

LITTLE BOY

I don't think so.

LITTLE MOMMA

Pain is a helluva drug. Is it the only way you're going to learn?

LITTLE BOY

I don't know.

LITTLE MOMMA

For someone as smart as you are you don't know anything when someone asks you something about yourself. If I tell you something important pay attention because this world doesn't hold back.

LITTLE BOY

Do you think I'm a sucker?

LITTLE MOMMA

No.

LITTLE BOY

Tell me the truth.

LITTLE MOMMA

Listen you have a big heart, and you are a good person in a city that eats good people with big hearts. People are going to use your kindness against you.

LITTLE BOY

Not me. I can dip and dodge them.

LITTLE MOMMA

Little Boy you are as green as a cucumber. This is the Queen City. You ain't dipping them and they're hard as hell to dodge. The best thing you can do is avoid them. Leave here and never come back.

LITTLE BOY

I haven't had any problems yet.

LITTLE MOMMA

Because you're broke. They can't see you yet. But they will as soon as they recognize that you are the prize.

LITTLE BOY

What does that mean?

LITTLE MOMMA

As soon people see you as a way out you won't have to look for anyone, they will find you.

LITTLE BOY

It's like that?

LITTLE MOMMA

It's just like that. Sounds crazy but it's true. You are too smart to stay here. Once you figure a way out, these broads are going to know you did. When that happens watch out.

LITTLE BOY

Watch out for what?

LITTLE MOMMA

The sick, the lame, the lazy, the deaf, the dumb, and the crazy. You care too much. You feel for others. That's how they will get to you. You got to turn that off. See the world because you belong to the world. Find someone else that's cool but don't let anyone make you believe they're the prize. Leave this city. Promise me that.

LITTLE BOY

I promise.

LITTLE MOMMA

I'm for real. There's nothing here but snakes.

LITTLE BOY

I said I promise.

LITTLE MOMMA

I know. So, what did this invisible man say to you? Because all I saw when I approached you was you standing there talking to yourself.

LITTLE BOY

I swear to you he was sitting right here, and we were talking for a long time.

LITTLE MOMMA

About?

LITTLE BOY

He spoke in riddles. Girl I was confused.

LITTLE MOMMA

Little Boy. What am I going to do with you? Focus.

LITTLE BOY

He said when life throws me curves, I duck inside myself. I shut down.

LITTLE MOMMA

True.

LITTLE BOY

Then he told me to stop worrying about being poor and focus on sharing who I am with the world.

LITTLE MOMMA

He said that?

LITTLE BOY

He said a lot of things.

LITTLE MOMMA

How did he close the conversation?

LITTLE BOY

As I understood him and I'm loosely paraphrasing here. How you feel effects how you think. How you think effects what you say. What you say or don't say defines how others treat you. He told me I can write my story or let others write it for me.

LITTLE MOMMA

Powerful words. You were talking to someone.

LITTLE BOY

I told you I was. I thought today was just about buying three pair of pants and three shirts.

LITTLE MOMMA

What?

LITTLE BOY

Nothing. Just thinking out loud.

LITTLE MOMMA

You ready to go?

LITTLE BOY

Yeah, I got what I came for.

LITTLE MOMMA

I got you something.

LITTLE BOY

You did? Why'd you do that? You have a baby to take care of.

LITTLE MOMMA

I know that. I'm handling my business. Remember you were the first baby I took care of? You really needed something to pick you up. Tell me if you like them.

LITTLE BOY opened the bag and took out an Adidas box and opened it to find a fresh pair of white-on-white leather shell toe Adidas. Just like Radio's. His favorites. He had looked at them every time they came to the mall. Dreaming about them.

This was the first pair of sneakers he had ever owned that didn't come out of a K-Mart barrel. He held them, and cried, and LITTLE MOMMA sat him down and held him. No one knew him like she knew him. She was part mother, part sister, part friend, part protector, and part teacher. She was his universe. He had missed her so.

(BLACKOUT)
(END OF SCENE)

Act 2

Scene 3

BASEBALLS

SETTING: Saturday Night Fulton County Stadium.

AT RISE: LITTLE BOY is seated next to GRANDDAD in the right field bleachers watching their favorite team The Atlanta Braves battle the New York Mets.

GRANDDAD bought LITTLE BOY, a Dale Murphy jersey, and a baseball glove before the game, all the popcorn he desired and a hot dog with his favorite grape soda pop. This was baseball.

LITTLE BOY

Granddad thanks for the jersey. How did you know Dale Murphy was my favorite Braves player of all time?

GRANDDAD

Boy I listen to you. You don't think I do. But I do. He's a good ballplayer, but I wish you could have seen Hammering Hank play. He was something special. He wasn't flashy. He wasn't the fastest, but he was fast enough. He wasn't the strongest, but he was strong enough. He didn't waste any motion. He didn't talk much either. I loved that about him because I can't stand people that run their mouth. A man doesn't need to talk much in my book. He just needs to do what he said he was going to do. But that man could play the game like no other.

LITTLE BOY

The home run king. Were you here when he broke the record?

GRANDDAD

I couldn't make it. We were playing the Dodgers. I had to work. Even if I didn't have to work, I wouldn't have gotten in. There wasn't a ticket to be had in the whole world. Everybody who was somebody was here for that game. But we had it on the radio in the factory. All the Black fellas were so excited, but we knew how dangerous the situation was for him, his family and even ourselves. Those white boys wanted to kill this man for playing the game of baseball and if you were loose with the lips, they would try to take out their anger on you, just for rooting for him. They can make something so beautiful so ugly. I will never understand them people as long as I live.

LITTLE BOY

What kind of man would want to kill another man for playing baseball?

GRANDDAD

A savage. This is Georgia. They don't consider us people. They hold on to this hate like it's a badge of honor. Passing it down generation to generation like an inheritance. The game may be baseball, but it is so much more to them than that. It's their pride. Pride fuels hate. Hate is his oxygen. He needs it to feel alive. Most of them aren't living any better than us. I'm sure that really bothers them. The thought of being supreme automatically creates an unstable person. He can't comprehend a world a black man can outthink him. Because what does that mean for him and his sons if that is possible? It destroys everything they believe in. The white man must always let you know he's in charge even when he isn't. He has to let you know he can do things you can't. But never the right things. He wants you to know the evil he can do to you. Remind you that he can do it and get away with it because he's protected. They bombed a church right here in Atlanta and killed four little girls. What kind of monster kills little girls?

LITTLE BOY

Why is he like that?

GRANDDAD

Because he made a deal with the devil and does the devils bidding upon the Earth.

LITTLE BOY

What does he get for that?

GRANDDAD

A season to have his heaven on Earth.

LITTLE BOY

Why is his heaven everyone else's hell?

GRANDDAD

He don't see it that way.

LITTLE BOY

He will one day.

GRANDDAD

He might but I doubt it. I'll never know. This government doesn't want him to be better. It's bigger than him. He doesn't know he's the tool being used. Until I see something different this may be the best he can be, in a world that loves him, just as he is.

LITTLE BOY

Filled with all that hate? Why would the world love that and who would make a man like that?

GRANDDAD

I didn't make him. Talk to the man above. He knows everything.

LITTLE BOY

You ever ask him why he made him that way?

GRANDDAD

I haven't spoken to the Lord in a long time. This hate been going on so long you just stop praying. It never changes anything. I had to let it go and let it be. If you dwell on it too long and you begin to feel like we're cursed because it doesn't make any sense for a man to hate someone he doesn't know or to hate women and children and the elderly. It's an evil that has choked all the goodness out of life. We ain't living here. We're just surviving.

LITTLE BOY

But everyone thinks this is the best place in the world.

GRANDDAD

It is if you love money and hate people and don't give damn about the land.

LITTLE BOY

Is hate evil?

GRANDDAD

Evil is evil. There are things in this life that a man should absolutely hate with all his conviction. Like evil, because you can't make deals with the devil. That's all this country does. You watch. Before you get my age everything that was called evil will be called good and everything that was called good will be called evil. Mark my words. I put that on everything. You're going to watch this world go crazy. (GRANDDAD pointed to his head and gave LITTLE BOY the crazy sign.)

LITTLE BOY

Do you hate them?

GRANDDAD

I hate evil and when they're in their evil mind I can't come up with a good reason for the Good Lord to give them oxygen to breath. But I don't want to ruin this game for you. Root for Murphy. He's the captain of the team, he's a damn good ballplayer, he plays the game the right way, and I just bought that expensive jersey.

LITTLE BOY

Can we talk about this later?

GRANDDAD

Yeah, we can. I'll need a couple of beers when we do. Let's get back to baseball. Niekro is pitching today. He has that nasty knuckleball. Its filthy.

LITTLE BOY

The ball is dirty?

GRANDDAD

Yeah, to the batters and the catcher it's extremely filthy. The ball could go anywhere after he throws it. Benedict is going to work today.

LITTLE BOY

The catcher?

GRANDDAD

Yeah, he is going to earn this game check. The ball has no spin on it so the catcher can only guess where it ends up.

LITTLE BOY

That sounds crazy. I have never seen the knuckleball before.

GRANDDAD

You won't see today either from back here.

LITTLE BOY

You are right about that I can't see anything but the outfielders numbers.

GRANDDAD

What's the name on the scoreboard?

LITTLE BOY

I can't tell.

GRANDDAD

What's the first letter?

LITTLE BOY

G?

GRANDDAD

Boy you are blind as a bat.

LITTLE BOY

Bats don't need good eyes, they use echolocation. They can get this close to you and never hit you.

(LITTLE BOY covered GRANDDAD'S face with his glove.)

GRANDDAD

It's a figure of speech Little Boy. Like deaf as a post. Don't be so literal all the time. It throws off the conversation. Don't do that thing with the glove in my face either. That's disrespectful. How's school going?

LITTLE BOY

It's going OK. I'm getting used to it.

GRANDDAD

I bet you are. Brett Butler is on first with no outs. I think he's about to steal second.

LITTLE BOY

Yeah, he's got some wheels on him.

GRANDDAD

You know stealing is a lot like lying. Every now and then you're going to get caught.

LITTLE BOY

Metaphors?

GRANDDAD

No, that's a fact Jack.

LITTLE BOY

Are we still talking about baseball?

GRANDDAD

Of course. We're at a baseball game.

LITTLE BOY

It doesn't seem like we're talking about baseball.

GRANDDAD

I am. What about you?

LITTLE BOY

I'm mostly listening.

GRANDDAD

Hypothetical question. What if you were Joe Torre and you had a ball player who drew ball four yet refused to leave home plate and take first base because he wants to hit a homerun. What would you do with him?

LITTLE BOY

I don't know. Kick him in the pants maybe. That sounds crazy why wouldn't he leave home and take the base?

GRANDDAD

My thoughts exactly. Why wouldn't Little Boy leave my home and take the base?

LITTLE BOY

I don't think we're talking about baseball anymore.

GRANDDAD

No screaming eagle shit. What am I talking about?

LITTLE BOY

School.

GRANDDAD

You're getting warm? Go on.

LITTLE BOY

I haven't gone in two weeks. How did you find out? I was throwing the letters away.

GRANDDAD

They called my job boy. Why did you quit?

LITTLE BOY

A gang of men followed me home from school.

GRANDDAD

A gang of men. I know you aren't the only one from the neighborhood that walks to school. You better come better than that or we are going to have some bigger problems right here. Do you want to see your Granddad get locked up for disorderly conduct? You want America to see me put some hands on you?

LITTLE BOY

No. Here's what happened. The first day of school I'm sitting in the auditorium waiting for someone to get me and take me somewhere to talk to somebody about something.

GRANDDAD

That didn't tell my anything.

LITTLE BOY

Hold on Granddad. I'm setting the scene. But this big girl. I mean man sized girl came in the auditorium and pointed in my direction and screamed the B word followed by I'm going to come over there and F you up.

GRANDDAD

Get on with the matter.

LITTLE BOY

I was in the third row. She lunges over the first row and in my direction. I closed my eyes and braced myself. But she grabbed the girl in the second row who had been tying her shoes. I never saw her. All I saw were her feet flying as she was pulled over two rows. Followed by fists. After witnessing that I stood up. Walked to the exit. Left the building and started walking to your house. About midway this gang of dudes wearing shirts like Winnie the Pooh started whistling at me and then they started following me.

GRANDDAD

Nobody would have been following you if you had kept your ass in school.

LITTLE BOY

True but I had already left. I have never had grown men cat calling me. I was like what the.... So, I started walking fast because these Pooh Bears had muscles. I knew couldn't outrun them. They were on me Granddad. I hit the corner of your street and I booked it to the house. I wasn't leaving this house again without you. Why wouldn't I take the base? There were about twelve balls out there between me and the bag. That's the whole truth Granddad.

GRANDDAD

Thanks for not lying to me. You know I can't deal with that. Twelve balls between you and the base. That was kind of funny. I thought you was thinking about going to the Marines.

LITTLE BOY

I am in the delayed entry program.

GRANDDAD

Tell me this. How in the hell are you going to graduate from boot camp when you won't go to school because you're scared of girls?

LITTLE BOY

That's different.

GRANDDAD

How's that different? In boot camp you got to get up every day and do something that you don't want to do.

LITTLE BOY

Granddad, I want to jump out planes, shoot guns, travel the world, and meet the ladies. It's just twelve weeks.

GRANDDAD

It will be the longest twelve weeks of your life. If you can't survive one day of Washington High, how are you going to survive that?

LITTLE BOY

I am not used to this. We didn't have fights in my school, and I rode the bus.

GRANDDAD

I am not a bus driver. I suppose you want to go home now. Is that what you're going to do when the D.I. gets in your face? You're going to quit because it's not what you're used to. Because you aren't used to people screaming and cussing at you? Making you do thing you don't want to do. I don't see how you're going to make it boy. I don't see it.

LITTLE BOY

Great so you think I'm a loser too. My own grandfather. I didn't come all the way down to Georgia to hear that. That's why I left the Queen City.

GRANDDAD

I didn't say that. I don't see how it's possible to graduate if you quit when it gets tough. That don't seem very Marine like to me.

LITTLE BOY

I need toughness. I'm not a quitter and I'm not a fool. I couldn't fight off a gang of men by myself and that school is not an option. It's a prison. Yes, I want to go home. I'm going to the Marines, and I don't care if no one believes I can do it. I believe I can do it. That's all that matters when it's all said and done. Right? I may not be the toughest but I'm tough enough.

GRANDDAD

OK I'll get you a ticket. Get you back home safe. Are you sure that's what you want boy? What we're not going to do is play this game again. You're just homesick.

LITTLE BOY

Yes, I'm sure.

GRANDDAD

Alright let's watch the game now.

LITTLE BOY

Yeah, let's watch the game Granddad.

GRANDDAD

Who's up now?

LITTLE BOY

The Braves.

GRANDDAD

This pitcher has thrown nothing but balls.

(LITTLE BOY cracked up laughing.)

GRANDDAD

What's so funny?

LITTLE BOY

Balls.

GRANDDAD

Twelve balls. (GRANDDAD chuckled.) Kids today.

(PEANUTS GET YOUR PEANUTS!)

(BLACKOUT)
(END OF SCENE)
(END OF ACT)

Act 3

Scene 1

A MAN AND A MULE

SETTING: D-WILL swings by to pick up LITTLE BOY. He's going to take him to meet a man who will talk to them about a mule.

AT RISE: D-WILL rings the doorbell at #8 and LITTLE BOY walks out to meet him.

LITTLE BOY

Man, what's up? Why you got me up this early? What's so important?

D-WILL

Nothing, I need you to take a walk with me.

LITTLE BOY

Where? The last time I went "walking" with someone I almost got my arm broke.

D-WILL

T-Dot told me about that. Why did the two of you walk to the Southside with one bike? Let me guess they thought you were stealing bikes.

LITTLE BOY

You came over here to diss me and invite me on a date.

D-WILL

Nah it ain't like that. We're not going on the South Side and we're not taking bikes because you don't have one. Problem solved.

LITTLE BOY

Where are we going and what are we going to do?

D-WILL

We're going to see a man about a mule.

LITTLE BOY

What the hell does that mean? Are you high?

D-WILL

No.

LITTLE BOY

I don't believe you. Run the jewels.

D-WILL

Why?

LITTLE BOY

You know why. Rabbit ear those pockets.

D-WILL

Aaight relax. (D-WILL pulls out the lining of his pockets)

LITTLE BOY

What's that?

D-WILL

I don't know how that got there. It's not mine. I swear to you.

LITTLE BOY

Righttttt.

D-WILL

I swear I didn't know it was there, but I can't take it where we're going. Let's just blaze so I can get my mind right. Then I can answer all your questions.

LITTLE BOY

Cool I got a forty and two slices of cold pizza from last night.

D-WILL

Lunch it is.

(Three hours later.)

LITTLE BOY

Spill the beans. Straight no chaser.

D-WILL

I'm going downtown to see a recruiter.

LITTLE BOY

A what?

D-WILL

A recruiter. You know the dudes that come to your school in the undercover vehicles with the corny uniforms and the shiny shoes. They feed you a bunch of lies and hit on all the girls.

LITTLE BOY

They sound like squares.

D-WILL

Bingo.

LITTLE BOY

Never heard of them. We don't play that at Honors.

D-WILL

They're looking for killers not bookworms.

LITTLE BOY

So, what ya saying? Smart people can't kill people?

D-WILL

They can but like a smart evil villain they have to make a plan, practice the plan, scrap the plan, make a new plan, and then they're dead.

LITTLE BOY

Anyway, what are you going down there to do? Sign your name in blood?

D-WILL

I'm going to go and learn how to make some money, see the world, go to school, smash girls from around the world, and get the hell out. I'm one and done.

LITTLE BOY

You got it all figured out. How do you know all this?

D-WILL

They come to my school all the time and I have an uncle who was a Marine.

LITTLE BOY

Those dudes are just throwing hooks in the water. Whoever bites, bites. You ain't nothing special to them.

D-WILL

No, they stepped straight to me. Killers know killers.

LITTLE BOY

Oh, you're a killer now. Where are the notches on your belt Quick Draw? That recruiter is probably a combat photographer or some other type of paperclip bandit.

D-WILL

Paperclip bandit. That's funny.

LITTLE BOY

How much are they paying?

D-WILL

A lot. Something like $700 - $800 a month. Free room. Free food. Free medical. Free dental. What more do I need?

LITTLE BOY

There are no free sandwiches. I guarantee there's a hook somewhere. What are you going to do with $800 a month?

D-WILL

Brews and booty.

LITTLE BOY

By yourself?

D-WILL

No, with my homie.

LITTLE BOY

What homie?

D-WILL

You. That's why I need you to take this walk. They got this thing called the buddy program and delayed entry. We sign up now and go later.

LITTLE BOY

The hook. I knew you was up to something. You trust these hustlers?

D-WILL

They can't hustle a hustler.

LITTLE BOY

You can't hustle a hustler. Hmmmm. Let's remember those words when we get back today.

D-WILL and LITTLE BOY enter the recruiting station nicer than nice. They had to walk the gauntlet of recruiters to get to the Marine Corps office.

AIR FORCE RECRUITER

Can I help you?

D-WILL

No, you cannot Skip.

ARMY RECRUITER

What brings you two in today?

LITTLE BOY

Not you Jeff.

NAVY RECRUITER

You boys look like you want to sail the seven seas?

D-WILL

Not wearing that bullshit.

COAST GUARD RECRUITER

Fellas.

LITTLE BOY

Fellas. I don't know what you are, but I know I don't want any parts of guarding the coast. They should have put you first.

COAST GUARD RECRUITER

Damn Jar Heads.

LITTLE BOY

Excuse me.

COAST GUARD RECRUITER

Staff Sergeant White you got two fish out here.

D-WILL

Who the hell is Simon Bar Sinister calling a fish?

LITTLE BOY

Must be recruiter talk. I'm sure it's an insult. He thinks we're stupid.

D-WILL

Yo we ain't stupid man.

STAFF SERGEANT WHITE

D-Will what's going on? Don't worry about Timmy. He's like that with everyone. You made it and you brought a buddy with you. What's your name young man?

LITTLE BOY

Little Boy.

STAFF SERGEANT WHITE

Why so serious? All fire no smoke. I like that. Little Boy it is. Nice to meet you. Glad you could make it too. Here's my card. Put it in your pocket. Don't lose it.

(STAFF SERGEANT BLACK sticks his head out of the office and into the public area and beckons STAFF SERGEANT WHITE to come into the office.)

STAFF SERGEANT BLACK

I heard Timmy yelling fish in the lobby. You know I need a bone this month.

STAFF SERGEANT WHITE

They're still in high school. They can't ship but you can run one of them on delayed entry.

STAFF SERGEANT BLACK

That's better than a doughnut. Won't stop the bleeding but it is a conversation starter. I'll take it. I need to get the captain off my ass.

STAFF SERGEANT WHITE

He is a douche bag. If that dude found an Irish Pennant, he'd pull it until your shirt fell off. Listen you can take his buddy. He said his name was Little Boy.

STAFF SERGEANT BLACK

Man stop lying. Who would name their kid that?

STAFF SERGEANT WHITE

I shit you not. That's what he said.

STAFF SERGEANT BLACK

Little Boy. OK. $100 dollars that ain't his name.

STAFF SERGEANT WHITE

I'll take that. What have we learned on these streets?

STAFF SERGEANT BLACK

The crazier something sounds the more likely it is to be true.

(LITTLE BOY and D-WILL were getting a little paranoid with the wait. The two recruiters re-entered the Common area.)

STAFF SERGEANT WHITE

Gents I gotta couple of treats for you. Which one of my cool ass posters do you like?

LITTLE BOY

I like that one of them running out of that green thing on the beach.

STAFF SERGEANT WHITE

That's an AAV my man. Amphibious Assault Vehicle. We can attack you from the air, the ground, and the sea. You want to ride one of those from the ship to the shore?

LITTLE BOY

In the water? That looks like a bathtub on wheels. Count me out.

STAFF SERGEANT WHITE

Which one do you like?

D-WILL

I want to fly. Give me that plane joint.

LITTLE BOY

You hate heights.

(LITTLE BOY looked puzzled at D-WILL.)

D-WILL

I want to fly man. Something wrong with that. (D-WILL did not realize he was shouting.)

LITTLE BOY

Yo You're yelling.

D-WILL

I am.? Oh shit. Oh. That picture got me hyped.

STAFF SERGEANT WHITE

I have one more treat for you. We call this instant moto. Staff Sergeant Black. Run the movie.

(LITTLE BOY and D-WILL sat and watched the movie as the two recruiters entered the office.)

STAFF SERGEANT BLACK

Fresh fish.

STAFF SERGEANT WHITE

Yeah, and they're faded. They could jump in and fall right out the damn boat. We're going to have to work with them before they ship.

STAFF SERGEANT BLACK

True. Where are they from?

STAFF SERGEANT WHITE

The Gardens.

STAFF SERGEANT BLACK

I heard they got some fine women down there.

STAFF SERGEANT WHITE

Man, I'm not trying to hear that. I got six months left on this bag. I'm doing my time and never looking back at this joint. This city is a dive.

STAFF SERGEANT BLACK

More for me. (The two recruiters re-entered the public area.)

STAFF SERGEANT WHITE

What do you think? Pretty motivating right? It gets me every time. Right here.

(STAFF SERGEEANT WHITE grabbed his crotch and LITTLE BOY and D-WILL laughed out loud.)

STAFF SERGEANT WHITE

Marine Corps!

LITTLE BOY

Is boot camp going to be like that?

STAFF SERGEANT BLACK

You damn skippy. We train hard and we play hard. But we're one big family. Light greens and dark greens. All getting along. We're going to treat you with firmness and give you all the dignity and respect you deserve.

D-WILL

That's good because if someone gets all up in my face. They might get these hands.

STAFF SERGEANT WHITE

Easy killer. They got the cure for what ails you. We're here to convince you to become the best you that you can be. We find civilian recruits and they make Marines. The finest fighting force that has ever existed on this Earth. You want to be part of that. Don't you? I see that fire in your eyes. Look at their eyes Staff Sergeant Black.

STAFF SERGEANT BLACK

Damn. I see it too. Let me see your war face.

D-WILL

What's that?

STAFF SERGEANT BLACK

The last thing the enemy sees before you slash and dash them to pieces. I want you to stare at that window and scream loud enough to shatter it.

D-WILL

Ahhhhhhhhhhhhhhhhh!!!!!!

STAFF SERGEANT WHITE

Little Boy. What's up? I know you got more fire than that. You're sounding a little weak.

(STAFF SERGEANT WHITE dropped $20 on the desk.)

LITTLE BOY

AHHHHHHHHHHHH!!!!!!!!

STAFF SERGEANT BLACK

D-Will you gonna let him show you up. We're stone-cold killers over here. Hit him with a kill.

(STAFF SERGEANT BLACK dropped his own $20 bill on the table.)

D-WILL

KILLLLLLLLLLLLLLLLLLLLL!

Five minutes later. LITTLE BOY and D-WILL are drained and suddenly sober with massive headaches. The two recruiters' smirk and pick up their money and place it back in their pockets. Well played. Well played.

LITTLE BOY

Boot camp looked pretty easy. What will I do after that?

STAFF SERGEANT BLACK

We have military occupational specialties. You might call them careers. Look at this pamphlet and let me know if you see something you're interested in.

LITTLE BOY

I want to work smart not hard. I want to learn a skill I can use when I get out. I'm no lifer. If I go, I'm four and out.

STAFF SERGEANT BLACK

You might like electronics. That's where the brainiacs hang out. If you score well on the ASVAB I can get you into that. You are eighteen, right?

LITTLE BOY

No, I'm seventeen.

STAFF SERGEANT BLACK

Not a problem. You will need your mother to sign one of my release forms so you can get in the program. That is if you're ready. Are you ready young man?

LITTLE BOY

Hell yeah. I'm a killer.

STAFF SERGEANT BLACK

That's what I'm talking about. Fill this out and I'll give your mother a call next week.

(LITTLE BOY filled out the form and handed it back to STAFF SERGEANT BLACK.)

STAFF SERGEANT BLACK

Well, I'll be damned.

STAFF SERGEANT WHITE

What?

STAFF SERGEANT BLACK

His name is Little Boy.

(STAFF SERGEANT BLACK reached into his wallet and grabbed five $20 bills.)

STAFF SERGEANT BLACK

Hand that to Staff Sergeant White for me.

(LITTLE BOY took the money from STAFF SERGEANT BLACK and handed it to STAFF SERGEANT WHITE who chuckled and placed it in his wallet.)

STAFF SERGEANT WHITE

Well gents that concludes our business for the day. I know you two studs have a couple of hot dates with the ladies lined up. After you let them know, you're going to the Marines, you'll have to fight them off. We'll be reaching out to your mothers next week so make sure you tell them you were here today so it's not a surprise. You copy?

(LITTLE BOY and D-WILL nodded, shook hands with the recruiters and left the office.)

COAST GUARD RECRUITER

Show me your war face?

D-WILL

I'm about to show you these nuts Timmy.

AIR FORCE RECRUITER

We can rest now the Marines are here.

LITTLE BOY

Yeah, aim low.

NAVY RECRUITER

You do know that Marines fall under the Department of the Navy.

D-WILL

Man go put on some real pants.

ARMY RECRUITER

Alas two more jar heads. What did they promise you?

LITTLE BOY

Your Ole Lady.

ARMY RECRUITER

What did you say?

LITTLE BOY

YOUR. OLD. LADY.

STAFF SERGEANT WHITE

Stan.

ARMY RECRUITER

Yeah.

STAFF SERGEANT WHITE

Let em go.

D-WILL

What the hell does alas mean?

LITTLE BOY

Shit you got me. My buzz is gone. My head is pounding and all I got is this corny ass poster.

D-WILL

We got the green weenie.

LITTLE BOY

The green weenie. That's funny. They got us.

(The fish were exiting the boat.)

(BLACKOUT)
(END OF SCENE)

Act 3

Scene 2

BITTERSWEET

SETTING: D-WILL's house in the New Gardens. A week before LITTLE BOY and D-WILL leave for the Island.

AT RISE: D-WILL and LITTLE BOY walk into the surprise party.

THE GATHERING

SURPRISE!!!!!!

LITTLE BOY

Hear ye. Hear ye. My faithful subjects. Who have gathered around to honor me. Where art thy throne?

LITTLE MOMMA

Little Boy you are so silly.

D-WILL

Appreciate it family. We can't do it without you.

LITTLE BOY

No really there's no throne.

ROBIN

Little Boy, I'll find somewhere for you to sit so we can talk.

BABY BOY

Little Boy, we got you a cake for your birthday. I picked it out. Let me show you.

(LITTLE BOY and BABY BOY went into the kitchen.)

LITTLE BOY

I can tell. Thanks Baby Boy. I appreciate it. You did good.

(BABY BOY dapped him up.)

MOM

Hey everyone let's gather around to sing Happy Birthday to Little Boy.

THE GATHERING

Happy Birthday to you. Happy Birthday to you. Happy Birthday. Happy Birthday to you. Happy Birthday to you. Happy Birthday.

LITTLE BOY

And the King said. Let the people eat cake. And it was so, and the people ate cake, and were merry.

MOM

Boy are you high?

LITTLE BOY

On life.

BABY BOY

Little Boy you forgot to blow out the candles.

LITTLE BOY

No, I didn't, I left that for you. Make a wish. Wish for something good.

BABY BOY

For real?

LITTLE BOY

For real.

(BABY BOY filled his cheeks with air and blew out the eighteen candles.)

LITTLE BOY

What did you wish for?

BABY BOY

A bike.

LITTLE BOY

For me?

BABY BOY

No for me.

LITTLE BOY

You gotta make a wish for me too or I'll have bad luck.

(BABY BROTHER closed his eyes and made a wish for LITTLE BOY.)

BABY BOY

I did it. But don't ask me what it is because it's a secret.

LITTLE BOY

When can you tell me?

BABY BOY

When you come back.

LITTLE BOY

Deal. I'll be back. You're the last of the Mohicans. I gotta see my little brother.

BABY BOY

The Mohicans.

LITTLE BOY

The last one in the tribe. I got something for you.

(LITTLE BOY pulled out $40 and gave it to BABY BOY.)

BABY BOY

Wow. I'm rich.

LITTLE MOMMA

Yeah, you are loaded Baby Boy.

T-DOT

Yo D-Will and Little Boy. Come here for second.

LITTLE BOY

This won't end well. What you up to T-Dot?

T-DOT

I got that fire.

D-WILL

Your mother is going to kill you if she catches you with that.

LITTLE BOY

We're only doing fire water tonight.

T-DOT

Smoke and flush man. This liquor will clean out your system. It's ninety proof. Gasoline.

LITTLE BOY

I'm pretty sure that's not how it works.

T-DOT

I got the fire from Gorilla Joe. I got the fire water from my Mom's stash.

D-WILL

You are really trying to die.

ROBIN

Ooooh T-Dot I'm going to tell.

LITTLE BOY

Robin, you don't want to do that.

ROBIN

Why don't I?

LITTLE BOY

Your mother will kill T-Dot. The party will be ruined. We're leaving next week. Do you really want to make everybody sad?

ROBIN

No. But T-Dot gets away with everything while I get blamed for every-thing and I'm tired of it.

LITTLE BOY

No one gets away with anything forever. Don't worry about that. Let's go in the hallway for a minute.

ROBIN

For what?

LITTLE BOY

So, we can talk. You said you wanted to talk.

(LITTLE BOY and ROBIN walk into the hallway.)

ROBIN

It's dark in here.

LITTLE BOY

I like the dark. Come here.

ROBIN

I'm right next to you.

LITTLE BOY

Closer.

ROBIN

Is this close enough

LITTLE BOY

Isn't this better than telling on T-Dot?

ROBIN

Way better.

LITTLE BOY and ROBIN went to France in the hallway. Their tongues intertwined, between heavy breathing, as their hands explored their bodies. Grinding.

T-DOT

And busted.

ROBIN

You better not say a word.

T-DOT

You neither.

ROBIN

Then we're even.

LITTLE BOY

Let's go drink.

T-DOT

Hold up. Why are you back here grinding my sister?

LITTLE BOY

Someone has to. Anyway, I was trying to keep you out of trouble.

T-DOT

Oh, I get it. You were taking one for the team.

LITTLE BOY

You could say that.

T-DOT

Bet it up.

D-WILL

Why y'all back here whispering in the dark?

T-DOT

Ask your boy he's back here making love scenes.

D-WILL

With who? You?

T-DOT

No.

D-WILL

Then who?

T-DOT

Ask your man Fifty Grand.

D-WILL

Little Boy who was it?

LITTLE BOY

I don't know anything. Let's go out back and catch a fade.

D-WILL

Let's do it.

(LITTLE BOY, D-WILL, and TD walk out back and poured some drinks.)

(One hour later.)

MA-WILL

Robin, where did the boys go?

ROBIN

They went out back.

MA-WILL

Get them. Tell them this is their party and its disrespectful to just disappear when people are here to see them.

(ROBIN went out back and saw the smoke around T-DOT's head before she smelled it.)

ROBIN

I know y'all not doing that here. Are you crazy? Talking about me ruining the party. Y'all trying to get a beatdown. D-Will your mother told me to get y'all. It's your party and you got guests.

T-DOT

You didn't see us.

ROBIN

Oh no. I'm not telling that lie. You're not getting me killed. I'm going to tell Ma-Will you're coming right behind me. Now y'all got five minutes, tops, to finish your little party with Mary Jane.

D-WILL

I swear she's a cop. You can't sneak anything past Robin.

T-DOT

Tell me about it. I live with her. Yo let's finish this bottle and hit this chaser.

D-WILL

Word. They got burgers, dogs, pizza, fries, and cake inside.

T-DOT

I got the munchies too.

LITTLE BOY

I bet you do.

(LITTLE BOY, D-WILL, and TD made their way back to the party inside. LITTLE BOY surveyed the room and saw CAT on one side of the room and LETTIE on the other. This was a potential problem.)

LETTIE

Hey Little Boy. Look at you all grown up. You're a man now. I don't know what to say to a man. I've never met one in these parts. You're about to see the world. You probably won't even think about me after you leave. Will you?

(CAT was taking it all in. Diary in hand.)

LITTLE BOY

Lettie, how'd you know about a party I didn't know about?

LETTIE

The Gardens talk.

LITTLE BOY

The Gardens or my sister?

LETTIE

A girl will never tell.

LITTLE BOY

What made you come?

LETTIE

If I didn't come to this party, I knew you'd leave without saying goodbye.

LITTLE BOY

I thought the last time we said goodbye was the last time we said goodbye.

LETTIE

I don't want to talk about that. You know I've been digging you for years Little Boy. I'm tired of playing this game. How long has it been? Five or six years. You are impossible to read. Then I have to hear about other girls. What am I supposed to do? Chase you down. Tie you up. I mean I would if that's what you like. Just playing. Relax. I know how your mind works. But you gotta tell me something. Why do you leave me guessing?

LITTLE BOY

Why are you different when other people are around?

LETTIE

You didn't answer one question. I could ask you the same thing. Don't trip. When it's you and your boys you don't have anything to say to me. Like you're embarrassed to be seen talking to me.

LITTLE BOY

I can't lie. You're right. I don't know why that happens. Peer pressure. Self-esteem. I could pick anything to make it sound right. But it isn't right. I like you, Lettie. But I didn't want you to know I liked you. I know it sounds crazy.

LETTIE

It is crazy. We let this go too long. But I got a birthday present for you.

LITTLE BOY

You bought me a gift?

LETTIE

I am the gift.

LITTLE BOY

Where's your bathroom at?

D-WILL

Over there.

LETTIE

You got another one?

D-WILL

Upstairs.

LETTIE

Thanks.

(LETTIE whispered into LITTLE BOY'S ear.)

LETTIE

I am going to go upstairs to the bathroom. Come up and see me in a few minutes

(LETTIE walked upstairs to the bathroom.)

D-WILL

You alright? You looked dazed.

LITTLE BOY

It just sunk in that I'm eighteen.

D-WILL

Yeah, you made it.

LITTLE BOY

I did. It feels so strange. Different shades of grey?

D-WILL

Huh?

LITTLE BOY

Thinking out loud.

(LITTLE BOY surveyed the room and saw CAT sitting on the couch talking to BABY BOY. She was occupied. He went upstairs and knocked on the bathroom door.)

LETTIE

Who is it?

LITTLE BOY

Little Boy.

LETTIE

Who?

LITTLE BOY

Little Boy.

LETTIE

Sorry can't let you in. I'm waiting for Little Man.

LITTLE BOY

Stop playing.

(LETTIE opened the door.)

LETTIE

Get in here and be quiet.

LITTLE BOY

Why'd you take all your clothes off?

LETTIE

Because I'm about to make love to a man.

LITTLE BOY

That's right.

LETTIE

I've never done this before.

LITTLE BOY

I've never been a man before. We're even.

LETTIE

I waited for you.

LITTLE BOY

I didn't know you were waiting.

LETTIE

You don't notice a lot of things. I was in love with you the moment I met you.

LITTLE BOY

You were twelve, I don't think that counts as love.

LETTIE

Don't mess up my moment. Take off your clothes.

LITTLE BOY

OK.

LETTIE

I'm going to give you a hickey.

LITTLE BOY

Why?

LETTIE

Because you're mine.

(LITTLE BOY and LETTIE found a way to fit five years of sexual tension into seven minutes. It was the greatest seven minutes of their young lives.)

LETTIE

I'm going to leave first. I'm going home now. I know you still got people to see. Throw a rock at my window when you're finished playing around. We're not done. I'll be waiting for round two.

LITTLE BOY

Me too. Was it good?

LETTIE

Yes, I'm a woman now.

(They laughed and LETTIE kissed LITTLE BOY long and passionately then left the bathroom.)

D-WILL

Where you been?

LETTIE

Upstairs bathroom.

D-WILL

Doing what?

LETTIE

Using the bathroom.

D-WILL

Where's Little Boy? Everyone's looking for him.

LETTIE

I don't know.

D-WILL

Are you sure?

LETTIE

Pretty sure.

D-WILL

Righttttt.

LETTIE

I gotta run. If I don't see you before you leave. Take care of him. You both have to make it out of here. Everyone is looking. People know you can make it. But most people don't think Little Boy's has a chance. They won't tell him but that's what they believe. They don't know him like I know him. He's special. Always has been. You are too. If he likes you, it's because there's something good in you. I know y'all can do it if you stick together. Don't let nothing happen to him tonight. We are having a night cap.

D-WILL

A night cap. Something must have happened during the day. I thought you didn't know where he was at. Y'all grown now.

LETTIE

He's a man and he just made me a woman. Bring him back alive.

D-WILL

That's my man. I got him.

(LETTIE left D-WILL'S house and LITTLE BOY came downstairs.)

D-WILL

Where you been?

LITTLE BOY

In the bathroom.

D-WILL

Yeah, the bathroom. Cat has been looking all over for you.

LITTLE BOY

Where is she?

D-WILL

In the kitchen.

(LITTLE BOY walked into the kitchen and sat at the table across from CAT.)

CAT

Where were you?

LITTLE BOY

Upstairs.

CAT

Where upstairs?

LITTLE BOY

In the bathroom.

CAT

With whom?

LITTLE BOY

Nobody.

CAT

Why are you lying? You said you'd never lie to me Little Boy. I heard y'all. Why do I get the short end of the stick? I've never lied to you, and I've been your best friend.

LITTLE BOY

Listen, I try to keep everybody happy. Do you know how hard that is?

CAT

I don't because I don't try to do that. I am good to whoever is good to me. It's about loyalty, Little Boy. That means everything to me. I am mad but I'm not jealous. I know I'm too young for you. I brought you a card. I want you to open it and read it before you get on the plane. My mother said you're going to need something to make you get on the plane. To get you to the island. She helped me write it.

LITTLE BOY

You told your mother about me.

CAT

She's always known about you. I didn't have to say a word.

LITTLE BOY

She knows we're friends, right?

CAT

Yes, but she also knows I like you a lot and she respects you because you're my best friend and you kept it there.

LITTLE BOY

You like me?

CAT

Yes, I like you. I wait for you every morning and you're the last person I see before I go in the house at night. You taught me so much about life. You didn't have an easy life. But you're not a quitter. You found a way out at eighteen. I just hope it doesn't cost you everything even if it costs you me.

LITTLE BOY

Cat, if you were eighteen, I would scoop you up right now and we'd see the world. There's no one around here like you. Don't spend your time down here in these Gardens when I'm gone. I want you to get out of here too and never look back.

CAT

I won't. Can I kiss you before I leave?

LITTLE BOY

Yes.

(LITTLE BOY popped in a fresh mint and CAT walked around and sat in his lap. She kissed him like she'd never see him again.)

CAT

I hope this memory lasts forever. Walk me to the door. My Mom is waiting outside.

(LITTLE BOY walked CAT to the front door.)

LITTLE BOY

Thanks for being my best friend, Cat. You're beautiful inside and out. Don't let anyone take that away from you.

CAT

I won't. I'll always love you. I mean like you. I gotta go Little Boy. Saying goodbye to you is much harder than I thought it would be.

CAT couldn't hold back the tears. LITTLE BOY came outside and held her and whispered words no one could hear nor would ever hear. Then she turned and walked slowly towards her mother's car.

MOM

You, OK?

LITTLE BOY

No. I'm not. I feel everything right now.

MOM

Your baby brother is trying to hold it together.

LITTLE BOY

Tell him to come here.

MOM

OK.

(BABY BOY walked out the door with tears streaming down his face.)

LITTLE BOY

Whoa little man what's going on? Why so many tears?

BABY BOY

I don't want you to go.

LITTLE BOY

Let's go sit on the bench. I'm not going forever.

(LITTLE BOY and BABY BOY walked to the bench and took a seat.)

BABY BOY

But you're never going to live here again.

LITTLE BOY

How do you know that?

BABY BOY

I just do.

LITTLE BOY

I'm always going to be your brother though. When you need me the most, I'll be there for you.

BABY BOY

Why do you have to leave?

LITTLE BOY

If I don't leave. None of us will leave. This city is a graveyard. You're going to leave to. Even if I have to come get you.

BABY BOY

You promise.

LITTLE BOY

I promise.

BABY BOY

When are you coming back?

LITTLE BOY

In October.

BABY BOY

Will you be a Marine then?

LITTLE BOY

I'm already a Marine. They just don't know it yet. I'll always be your brother. Marine or no Marine. Remember that. You hear me? Keep your head up.

BABY BOY

Yeah. I still don't want you to go.

LITTLE BOY

You know I got to.

BABY BOY

Yeah...

The two brothers sat on the bench and LITTLE BOY listened to BABY BOY talk. He was so full of life. Just getting started. One year younger than LITTLE BOY when he arrived in the Queen City. He could see the innocence in BABY BOY. The piece of himself that was missing. Life was bittersweet. His final thought. A prayer that no one would take BABY BOY's innocence from him. A prayer that he had paid the price and would be the last little boy with the blues in his tribe.

(BLACK OUT)
(END OF SCENE)
(END OF ACT)
(END OF PLAY)